SEX TAKES A HOLIDAY

THE BURGLAR ON THE PROWL • THE BURGLAR WHO COUNTED THE SPOONS • THE BURGLAR IN SHORT ORDER

KELLER'S GREATEST HITS

HIT MAN • HIT LIST • HIT PARADE • HIT & RUN • HIT ME • KELLER'S FEDORA

THE ADVENTURES OF EVAN TANNER

THE THIEF WHO COULDN'T SLEEP • THE CANCELED CZECH • TANNER'S TWELVE SWINGERS • TWO FOR TANNER • TANNER'S TIGER • HERE COMES A HERO • ME TANNER, YOU JANE • TANNER ON ICE

THE AFFAIRS OF CHIP HARRISON

NO SCORE • CHIP HARRISON SCORES AGAIN • MAKE OUT WITH MURDER • THE TOPLESS TULIP CAPER

COLLECTED SHORT STORIES

SOMETIMES THEY BITE • LIKE A LAMB TO SLAUGHTER • SOME DAYS YOU GET THE BEAR • ONE NIGHT STANDS AND LOST WEEKENDS • ENOUGH ROPE • CATCH AND RELEASE • DEFENDER OF THE INNOCENT • RESUME SPEED AND OTHER STORIES

BOOKS FOR WRITERS

WRITING THE NOVEL FROM PLOT TO PRINT TO PIXEL • TELLING LIES FOR FUN & PROFIT • SPIDER, SPIN ME A WEB • WRITE FOR YOUR LIFE • THE LIAR'S BIBLE • THE LIAR'S COMPANION

WRITTEN FOR PERFORMANCE

TILT! (EPISODIC TELEVISION) • HOW FAR? (ONE-ACT PLAY) • MY BLUEBERRY NIGHTS (FILM)

ANTHOLOGIES EDITED

DEATH CRUISE • MASTER'S CHOICE • OPENING SHOTS • MASTER'S CHOICE 2 • SPEAKING OF LUST • OPENING SHOTS 2 • SPEAKING OF GREED • BLOOD ON THEIR HANDS • GANGSTERS, SWINDLERS, KILLERS, & THIEVES • MANHATTAN NOIR • MANHATTAN NOIR 2 • DARK CITY LIGHTS • IN SUNLIGHT OR IN SHADOW • ALIVE IN SHAPE AND COLOR • AT HOME IN THE DARK • FROM SEA TO STORMY SEA • THE DARKLING HALLS OF IVY

SEX TAKES A HOLIDAY
Copyright © 1964, by Lawrence Block
Original Publication, writing as Howard Bond

All Rights Reserved. This book or parts thereof may
not be reproduced in any form, stored in any retrieval
system, or transmitted in any form by any means—
spoken, written, photocopy, printed, electronic,
mechanical, recording, or otherwise through any
means not yet known or in use—without prior written
permission of the publisher, except for purposes of
review.

Cover & Interior by JW Manus

A LAWRENCE BLOCK PRODUCTION

SEX TAKES A HOLIDAY

LAWRENCE BLOCK

THE CLASSIC EROTICA SERIES

Lust Weekend
Man for Rent
Of Shame and Joy
Passion Nightmare
Sex Takes a Holiday
Sin Bum
The Sin-Damned
Sin Hellcat
Sexpot!
Sin Master
Sintime
A Strange Kind of Love
So Willing
Trailer Trollop
Tramp
The Twisted Ones
The Wife-Swappers
A Woman Must Love

Chapter One

WHEN THE FASTEN SEAT BELTS sign went on, Mel Dalton stubbed out his cigarette in the ashtray and hooked his belt around his middle. He was a big man, tall, broad in the shoulders and thick in the waist, with legs like tree trunks. He looked out the window of the plane and saw the ground below.

Miami. Miami, and two weeks in the sun. Two weeks out of New York, two weeks away from Park Avenue. Two weeks during which he wouldn't have to think once of Fragile Frocks, Inc. Two weeks during which his partner could rob him blind, and, by the same token, two weeks during which he could do the same kind of cheating on the broad sitting next to him now.

The broad sitting next to him was his wife. He looked over at her now, a glimmering of distaste in his eyes. She was asleep, he saw. Put Mel Dalton on a plane and he had to work harder than the pilot. He sweated it out every mile of the way, waiting for the plane to conk out, waiting for some idiot with a bomb in his luggage to make Heaven the hard way, waiting for some burst of horror to end everything for him. A plane ride, minute for minute, was about as much fun for him as hanging.

But his bitch of a wife just closed her eyes and slept like a lamb.

Her seat belt wasn't fastened, he noticed. He reached over to fasten it, then abruptly changed his mind. The hell with it, he told himself. Let her leave it unhooked. Maybe, with a little luck, they would have a nice choppy landing and shake her up a little bit.

He sighed and looked at her again. That was one thing he had to admit. She was easy to look at. Susan Dalton was goddamn easy on the eyes. A tall blonde with skin so soft your heart pounded whenever you touched her. A body that gave a man lumps in his throat. Breasts that surged forward, firm and flawless, full and beautiful. Legs that were round and swollen at the thighs, tapering down gently to trim ankles and surprisingly tiny feet.

It was something to watch her walk. When she pranced around in a pair of those extra-high heels she was crazy about, it was really something to watch her walk. All of that beautiful body balanced precariously upon those very small feet, the feet wedged into high-heeled shoes, and the arch of her leg, and the sweet movement of her body, sweet poetry in motion—

Sure!

Terrific.

Mel grinned in quiet amusement. Half the men on earth would envy him, he knew. All he had to do was walk down the street with her on his arm and he could feel eyes trailing them, could imagine the thoughts that men were thinking. They all figured he was the luckiest son of a gun on earth. With a piece like that on his arm, he looked as though he must be on top of the world.

Sure.

But Mel Dalton knew better. Good to look at? Oh, none better than Sue when it came to that. But looking was all she was good for. When you touched her she turned cold as ice. When you kissed her she stood there and took it like a statue. And when you got her in the hay and got those magnificent legs apart and settled down for the ride, it was like making love to your own reflection in the mirror. She didn't move, she didn't feel, she didn't enjoy.

She was frigid. Not just partially frigid, liking it without getting all the way with it. No, she was a textbook case, a girl who didn't like it at all. She would put up with it when she had to, but that was about it. And she didn't even put up with it if she could avoid it. Given her choice, she'd rather pretend a headache or a back ache or a quick case of exhaustion—anything to keep him on his side of the bed and out of her pants.

After a while, he had gotten so that he stopped trying.

After a while he decided it just wasn't worth the effort. He wasn't a hot-pants kid who just wanted to get on and ride. He was a man, and he wanted a real woman under him, one who made a give-and-take relationship out of sex, one who gave as good as she got and loved it all the way. Sue might be built like a goddess, but she was about as bad in bed as it was possible to be. It just wasn't worth the effort to score with her. There was no kick.

THE PLANE TOUCHED DOWN on the runway. Mel braced himself, sure that the plane was going to scoot off the runway and go off like a firecracker. Instead, the giant jet taxied the length of the runway and pulled to a smooth stop. Just as he was unhooking his seat belt, Sue yawned and stretched and rubbed at her eyes with the back of her hand.

"Are we here?"

"We're here," he said.

"Mmmmm. I had a nice nap."

Good for you, he thought.

"I didn't have my belt fastened when we landed," she said. "You should have belted me, Mel."

I'd love to belt you, he thought. Right in the mouth.

They got off the plane. Outside, it was the sort of day that gladdens the heart of the Miami Beach chamber of commerce. The sun was high in the sky. There were no clouds. The air was warm, very warm. They walked to-gether to the terminal and waited until their baggage came from the plane to the baggage dock. Mel loaded their suitcase into a cab and they headed for the hotel.

They had reservations at the Banzai, one of the newer oceanfront hotels at the northern end of the Strip. Their cab headed north on Collins Avenue and Mel relaxed in the back seat and got a cigarette going. Miami Beach, he thought. Here we are. Two weeks of fun and sun, and he was going to crowd a lot of living into those two weeks.

In a way, it was a damned shame he had brought Sue along. She wouldn't be any good to him and she would only cramp his style. But he would have had a hell of a time taking the trip without her. This was easier. Let her swim around in the pool and sack out in a deck chair get-ting a good tan. In the meantime, he'd get more action in two weeks than he normally got in a year.

With any luck at all, Sue would never even realize he was playing around. But it didn't matter a hell of a lot if she happened to find out. What did he care? If she didn't like it, she could pack up and get out of his life. She wasn't any good to him the way things stood. It would be simpler and smoother if she could go on staying in the dark, but it didn't really matter one way or the other.

"We're here, Mac."

He looked up, abruptly pulled out of his reverie. The

cab had come to a stop in front of the Hotel Banzai. A doorman opened the door. Sue got out of the cab and he followed her, with the doorman scooping up their luggage and bringing up the rear.

On the way into the lobby, he couldn't take his eyes off his own wife. The most beautiful woman on earth, he told himself. There was no woman he had ever seen with a walk like that, no woman who made those unconscious movements with her rounded hips, no woman who looked so tremendously exciting in high heeled shoes.

But what good did it do?

None.

No good at all.

She was untouchable. Or, if she did let him touch her, the ultimate effect was like making love to a bottle of warm beer. There were times when the sight of her overwhelmed him, times when he was so hot and horny he couldn't hold back, times when he had to swallow his pride and beg her to let him have her. Each of those occasions was so unsatisfactory it left him swearing to have nothing more to do with her. She never responded, never acquiesced. She merely lay there like a dummy with a sick expression on her face and waited for him to finish and roll off of her. Then, as he lay panting, exhausted but unsatisfied, she would hurry at once to the bathroom as if she could not rest until she had washed the memory of his embrace from her soiled flesh.

A marriage like this was no marriage at all, Mel knew. Of course, she did all right as long as sex stayed out of the picture. She kept a good home, cooked well, entertained well, and was good to show off to his friends. But didn't a man have a right to expect more than that from his wife?

At the desk, he told them who he was. The clerk had his reservation on file. Mel signed the registration card and a bellboy led them to their room. The room was a large one with a view of the ocean. It had twin beds, of course. That was inevitable. Sue would no more go for a double bed than she would go for sex itself.

When the bellhop had taken his tip and departed, Mel sat down on the edge of his bed and lit a cigarette.

"Well," he said, "we're here."

"I know. And the weather's lovely."

He looked at her. She was hanging some of her things in the closet, standing with her profile to him, and he couldn't stop staring at the way her breasts thrust out against the fabric of her dress when she reached up to hang a dress on the bar in the closet. He let his eyes trail lingeringly down her body and felt desire rage in him like a fire in a dry forest.

Maybe he ought to just grab her whenever he wanted her, he thought. Maybe the caveman approach was what she needed. Maybe if somebody just picked her up and tossed her down and pulled her skirt up and slammed it into her she would learn what it was like to be a woman, a real woman! Maybe one good rape would turn the trick and make a woman out of her.

He rejected the thought. The caveman approach just wasn't his style, he knew. Besides, it would only turn Sue's stomach.

She finished unpacking and turned to him. "The trip exhausted me," she said. "I'm dished."

"Why? Just from sitting on a plane for a couple of hours?"

"I know, but—"

"And you slept all the way," he said.

"I'm still tired. Travelling always has that effect on me, Mel. Do you mind if I take a nap?"

He started to say something, then changed his mind. After all, what the hell did he care if she took a nap? He didn't want to spend a hell of a lot of time with her to begin with. Besides, if she was asleep for a couple of hours, he could use that time to scout around and see what kind of action the hotel had on tap.

That was one thing about the Miami hotels. If you couldn't find a woman without trouble, it meant you weren't trying. There were always a hell of a lot of broads on tap. Some of them played for money, and some of them played for fun, and some of them just played whenever they had the opportunity. But if you were looking for action, you sure as hell didn't have far to look.

"Go ahead," he told her.

"I think I'll take a shower first."

"Suit yourself."

"My skin's crawling from the flight. I must have perspired a lot in my sleep or something."

Nice romantic talk, he thought. She wouldn't put out, but she'd tell you about her sweat glands until you wanted to run and hide.

"Great."

"You don't mind?"

"Why should I mind?"

She sighed, set her cigarette down in the ashtray on the bedside table, and reached behind her back to get hold of the snap on her dress. The movement pushed her breasts forward until the two swollen orbs of succulent flesh threatened to burst through the front of the dress. Mel's eyes widened and he felt dots of perspiration on his forehead. He wanted to look away from her but he couldn't. She opened the dress and worked the zipper downward, then shrugged her shoulders so that the dress fell forward. She stepped out of it and hung it in the closet.

She pulled her lacy white slip over head and removed it. Her shoulders were creamy, her whole body soft and invitingly pink. Mel's mouth was dry and his hands were damp with perspiration.

"A few hours sleep will do me wonders, Mel."

"Sure," he said, running his tongue over his lips.

"Beauty sleep."

"You don't need it."

"Why?"

"Because you're beautiful."

If she appreciated the compliment, she gave no sign. She reached behind her for the bra clasp and had trouble with it. She backed up to him and asked him to help her. His hands were shaking. He tried to undo the bra without letting his fingers touch her flesh but this was impossible. When he touched the delicious smoothness of her body he thought he was going to go out of his mind with desire for her. He finally got the bra unhooked and tossed it over her shoulders so that it slipped down and fell to the floor.

Then he couldn't stand it any longer. With an awful sob he threw his arms around her and caught hold of her huge breasts in his large hands. He held them and squeezed them and his brain raced with fearful hunger. So soft and so firm and so smooth and so tremendously hugely big—

"Mel."

Her voice was cold and distant, cutting his passion like a sword chopping off his virile manhood.

"Mel, please. I told you I was tired."

"You're always tired," he managed to say.

"Mel—"

He dropped his hands. She turned to look at him, a scornful expression on her face. He tried to swallow but he couldn't get rid of the lump in his throat.

"You know I don't like to be grabbed like that. You act like an animal when you touch me like that. What kind of woman do you think I am, Mel?"

He almost told her. No woman at all, he wanted to say. A real woman would go out of her mind if a man grabbed her like that. A real woman would be down on that floor with her legs wide apart. A real woman would be panting like a truck horse. But she wasn't a real woman. She was a chunk of ice.

She walked from him now, unhooked her stockings from her garter belt. She sat on the edge of her bed and removed her high-heeled black shoes. He looked at her tiny feet and his mouth watered. Slowly, tantalizingly, she unrolled her stockings over her gorgeous legs and drew them off in turn.

Whew—

He was trembling. He reached for a cigarette, got it going. She was standing up now, removing first the garter belt and then the panties underneath it. He got a glimpse of her triangle of what ought be passionate yearning. His throat caught and he coughed on a lungful of smoke.

She didn't even seem to know he was there.

Downstairs, he thought. Downstairs, in the hotel bar, there would be a woman. A woman who would know how to make a man happy. A woman who might respond the way women were born to respond.

A woman who could make him feel like a man.

"Sue," he said.

She looked at him and he looked away from her. His urgent manhood stiffened furiously at the sight of her. She had an extraordinary body, and it was all he could do to keep himself from tossing her down on the rug and putting it to her whether she liked it or not, whether she was ready to let him or not.

"I think I'll go downstairs and get a drink or two."

"All right."

He turned from her, forcing himself to go. He opened the door and slipped out into the hallway, headed for the elevator. He had to have a woman, no matter what. And he had to have one pretty damned fast.

CHAPTER TWO

WHEN THE DOOR SLAMMED shut Sue Dalton sank down onto the bed and took a deep breath. She held it in her lungs for several moments, then let out the air in a gushing sigh. He was gone, thank God. She was alone. She could relax now.

Her breasts still remembered the touch of his hands, and she shivered unpleasantly at the recollection. Why did she stay with him? Because she was too scared to leave him, she thought. Because he made a good living and let her live a comfortable life. And she liked comfort. And because he usually left her alone, violating her flesh and invading her body only on rare occasions when his desires were too much for him.

Perhaps she shouldn't have undressed in front of him today, she thought. It was a foolish thing to do. Why provoke him with the sight of her flesh when she wasn't ready or willing to yield up possession of it?

Foolish, she told herself. And yet it was hard to avoid. It was almost as though she got some strange pleasure out of exciting him without letting him do anything about his excitement. The pleasure of watching him sweat. The pleasure of knowing that she had aroused him and know-ing, too, that he could do nothing to sate his urges, the urges she had awakened.

She went into the bathroom, turned on the water in the stall shower and adjusted it until the temperature was the way she liked it, as hot as she could possibly stand it. She slipped under the spray and closed the shower's glass door. The water rushed down upon her naked flesh and she gave herself up to the delightful fury of the spray.

A shower was a wonderful sensation, she knew. She relaxed completely now, letting the warm water drain ten-sion and exhaustion from her body. She had lied to Mel, of course. She wanted the shower, but she didn't plan to take a nap afterward.

She had better things to do.

She took a cake of soap, worked up a rich lather and massaged it into her creamy skin. She soaped her neck and shoulders, working the lather into her pores, soaping and rinsing until her skin was squeakily clean. She lath-ered her breasts and thrilled at the feeling as her hands manipulated and caressed her soap-slippery mounds of woman-flesh. Before, when Mel had touched her here, she had wanted to throw up. Now her own hands had a far different effect.

She felt her small pink nipples going stiff as pas-sion built up within her. She tweaked her nipples until they tingled deliciously, then held the full weight of her oversized breasts in her hands and squeezed them until they ached. Passion began to mount up within her body and she felt delicious tremors in the long muscles of her rounded thighs.

She soaped her belly, her legs. She reached around to lather her back, rinsed off, and then carefully and systematically soaped her bottom. Her rump was rounded deliciously. She cupped the sweet hemispheres of her buttocks and soaped them and soaped between them and felt her knees shake slightly.

Mel thought she was cold.

That was because he didn't know her, didn't know a thing about the fires that ranged within her. He could never ignite those fires, not in a million years. He could try to be tender or he could come on like an animal. It didn't matter. No matter how he approached her, she could never respond to him.

And for a simple reason.

He was a man.

And she was a lesbian.

She turned to face the shower's hot spray again, thrusting the lower part of her body forward so that the water lashed at her stomach and thighs. She lathered herself there and rinsed and soaped and rinsed and soaped and rinsed and felt passion build up within her like a hurricane sweeping down over the Florida beaches. She soaped and rinsed and knew that she could not stay in the room that afternoon. She had to get out, had to go to one of the special places, had to find someone who would treat her the way she wanted and needed and ached to be treated.

She had to find a woman.

It wasn't easy in New York. There were places, of course—gay bars where she could be fairly sure of finding a girl who was looking for the same thing that Sue was looking for. There were plenty of places like that. With Mel at the office all day she had plenty of opportunity to go to those places and find those girls and taste the sweet fruit of forbidden pleasure.

But she didn't like to go to those places in New York. New York was a big city, but it was her city. There were too many people there who knew her. She was always terribly nervous that one of her little trips to the gay bars would result in a meeting with someone who knew Mel. Then the game would be up. The idea of discovery terrified her, and so she kept her lesbian expeditions to a minimum in New York and only went out when the hunger got so bad that she couldn't contain herself any longer.

When that happened, she would give in and do what she had to do. A quick cab ride down to the Village. A drink or two at the bar of one of the lesbian haunts, waiting until some girl sized her up and decided she was worth a try. This usually didn't take long—she had the sort of face and body that appealed to both men and women, and whenever she went cruising the bars and looking for sex a girl approached her before too long.

Then a drink or two, and a snatch of conversation, and off to the lesbian's apartment. Then her clothes would be cast aside, and she would kiss and be kissed, would touch and be touched, and her whole body would go off on an endless shattering, stunning, jolting joyride to the end of the world.

It was always perfect with girls.

And it was always terrible with Mel.

Now the combination of her own sex-ridden thoughts and the lingering caresses her artful hands had applied to her own body had started a fire which refused to be kept under control. It was time, she told herself. She could slip out of the hotel. She could find a woman who wanted the same thing she wanted. And, while Mel went off to find some tramp to handle his passion, she would get her own thrills with a woman who knew how to give her pleasure.

She smiled at the thought. Here they were, on a two-week vacation in glorious sunny Miami Beach. And here, under the sun, snug in the warmth, they would both find the pleasures that their awful marriage compelled them to do without. Mel wanted women—he couldn't have her, not here and not in New York, but he could have all the other women he wanted and she couldn't care less.

And she could have her own weird kind of fun. Because no one knew her here, and she didn't have to worry about discovery. All she had to do was get her kicks.

She turned off the hot water now, letting the cold water lash at her body and seal her pores. The icy spray was almost too much for her to bear, but she stood it as long as she could, dancing from one foot to the other as the ice water teased her flesh. Then she turned it off altogether and slipped out of the shower and dried her lovely body with a nubby pink towel.

She dressed to perfection. She chose a lime-green dress with a neckline that plunged so low that it showed the tops of her glorious breasts. Under it she wore a half-bra of lacy black silk and matching black silk panties trimmed with sexy red fringe. She put on stockings and chose black pumps with three-and-a-half inch heels. They were so high she could barely walk in them, but she knew what wonders they did for her tiny feet and her long lovely legs.

She inspected herself in the mirror. Lovely, she told herself. She wished suddenly that she had a twin sister. What a frolic that would be, she thought. To have the chance to make love to another girl who looked just as she herself looked.

Small chance of that.

But she would have the next best thing.

She would have a woman.

And soon.

She dabbed perfume under each arm and between her bountiful breasts. She took a last fleeting look at herself in the mirror, then walked out of the room and down the hallway to the elevator. She rode downstairs and hesitated for a moment in the magnificent lobby, replete with potted palms and deep carpeting and ornate Oriental furnishing. The Banzai was a magnificent hotel, and she had to include it mentally in the list of benefits of being married to Mel Dalton. When you traveled with Mel, she knew, you traveled first-class. Money didn't matter. He spent it as though it was going out of style.

In the lobby, something drew her toward the cocktail lounge. She didn't want to go in there, because she was certain that Mel would be there and she didn't want to see him. But maybe he wasn't there, she thought. After all, he had left the room half an hour ago, and after the little teasing exhibition she had put on for him he would probably have been anxious to get past the preliminaries and rush on to the main event. With any luck at all, he would have found a girl by now, and instead of staying in the hotel bar he would be in a bedroom, getting what he couldn't get from his own wife.

So why not have one quick drink at the hotel bar?

The cocktail lounge was kept cooler than the lobby. She slipped into the darkened room and scanned the bar and tables quickly for a sign of Mel's presence. He did not seem to be there. She found her way to a small table backed by a bamboo room divider and sat down. A Chinese waiter came at once to take her order. She asked for a dry bourbon Manhattan. The waiter went away and she took a pack of cigarettes from her purse, put one in her mouth and lit it with a cigarette lighter. The lighter was silver, with her monogram done on one side in small diamonds. A birthday gift from Mel—gaudy, just as Mel himself was gaudy, but very expensive.

The waiter brought her drink. She sipped it and felt herself begin to relax pleasantly. The drink was gone almost before she knew it, and the waiter was at her elbow in an instant to ask her if she wanted another. She did, and he brought it to her.

Just as she raised her glass, she noticed the woman.

The woman was at the bar. She wore a very simple black dress, and her dark hair was bound back in a severe bun. Her forehead was high and broad, her lips quite pale, her eyes burning with an intense stare. Sue looked at her and looked away at once. Then, slowly, she let her eyes drag themselves back to the woman.

The woman was still looking at her.

And there was no mistaking the glance. Some women might not have recognized that long-drink look, but Sue had been around enough to read invitation in another woman's glance. The woman was like her, a lesbian. Right here in the same hotel, and gay as a magpie, and anxious to play.

Sue's blood surged through her veins. She looked at the woman and liked what she saw. Around twenty-nine or thirty, she guessed, give or take a year or two. Tall, and very well-built, with breasts that struggled to burst free from the confines of the severe black dress. Sue could imagine the way those breasts would feel in her hands, could imagine the tantalizing caresses of those pale lips. Her heart pounded and she felt weak all over.

Then, deliberately, she returned the woman's stare. Her lips curled into a half-smile of invitation. The woman picked up her drink and came quickly across the room to her. Sue's smile widened and the woman sat down at her table.

"I've been watching you," the woman said. Her voice was deep, husky with desire.

"I know."

"I haven't seen you here before."

"I just got here this afternoon."

"You're married?"

Sue looked at her wedding ring. "My husband's out for a while. Out chasing women."

"Oh? When he has someone like you?"

"He doesn't have me. Not if I can help it."

"I see."

"I thought you would."

The woman finished her drink, lit a cigarette. "My name is Kay," she said.

"I'm Sue."

"You know what I want, don't you?"

"I want the same thing."

"Does your husband know about you?"

"He thinks I'm frigid."

"Are you frigid, Sue?"

Her eyes flashed in sultry invitation. "Just try me," she murmured throatily. "Judge for yourself."

She felt Kay's hand on her thigh under the table. She gasped at the touch. The woman's hand was strong and competent and the woman seemed very sure of herself. Sue's smile remained. The woman's hand lifted the hem of her skirt and settled on her knee. She could feel the woman's fingers probing through her sheer nylon stocking. The hand crept higher, up past the top of the stocking, up onto the bare skin of her thigh. Sue began to tremble. It was almost impossible for her to sit still. The tops of her sweet thighs were already damp with the dew of love, and she wanted to grab Kay and have her right here, right here in the bar, just so she had her. It didn't seem to matter if the whole world watched.

Higher the hand moved.

Higher.

And Kay said, "No, I don't think you're frigid. I think you're very passionate, Sue."

"If you don't stop that—"

"Then what?"

"Then I'll go crazy. I need it so badly, Kay. Oh, I need it so badly."

"Come with me."

"Where?"

"My room."

"Are you staying here?"

"Yes. Come with me."

She had trouble getting to her feet. She was so shaky she thought she was going to fall apart at the seams. Kay threw bills on the table for their drinks and led the way out of the cocktail lounge. They headed straight across the lobby to the elevator and rode to the sixth floor.

Kay opened the door to her room with her key. They stepped inside, and the older woman shut the door and turned to her and took her in her arms. One of her hands went around Sue's waist. The other slipped quickly and deftly up under her skirt and found her at once and turned her bones to jelly. She sagged against Kay and panted furiously. She was on fire from head to toe and she couldn't wait.

Now, she thought. Now!

CHAPTER THREE

WHEN MEL WALKED INTO the bar at the Banzai, he figured that he'd have a quick drink or two and give the field the once-over. He didn't really expect to find any action right there in the hotel, not in the middle of the afternoon. But one drink would let him unwind a little, and then he could go outside and catch a cab and have the driver take him somewhere to find a woman. Miami Beach cab drivers were equipped to handle that sort of request. He might get himself hauled to one of the old-fashioned cathouses—there were still a few in operation in Southern Florida. Or the cabby might know some babe who did a thriving business at home. One way or another, Mel Dalton damn well intended to get his ashes hauled.

But, as it turned out, he didn't have to hunt a pimping cab driver. He didn't have to set a foot outside the hotel. All he had to do was take one step inside the cocktail lounge and he knew immediately that he would have to go no farther. The minute he saw the redhead on the end stool, he knew he had found precisely what he was looking for. And the minute she turned and met his eyes with her own, he knew it would be no problem. She was in the mood, and he was in the mood, and that, by George, was all it took.

He hurried across the room and took the stool next to her. She looked at him, her eyes bright. Her eyes were green, and they contrasted nicely with her tawny red mane. She was a big girl, big all over, especially big in the places where a girl was supposed to be big. Broad where a broad should be broad, he thought. She wore a green dress that matched her eyes. It was cut daringly low in front, low enough so that the deep valley between her large breasts showed plainly. Perfume wafted up from that valley and hit him between the eyes with the force of a pneumatic hammer.

The palms of his hands itched crazily. His mouth was dry, his throat tied in knots. The bartender came over, eyeing him quizzically. Mel had trouble ordering.

"I'll have J&B scotch on the bed," he blurted.

"Huh?"

"On the rocks," he corrected himself, feeling incomparably foolish. The bartender nodded sagely and went away to pour scotch over ice. He brought the drink back and Mel told him to give the lady a drink as well. She was on stingers. The bartender made her one and put it on Mel's tab. The redhead raised her glass appreciatively, took a small sip. Her lips were scarlet, her tongue pink and exciting. She turned to Mel and eyed him intently.

"They're real," she said.

"Huh?"

She looked down at her breasts, then raised her eyes to meet his once more. "You were looking at them hard enough," she said softly. "As if you didn't think they were all mine. I just wanted to reassure you, sugar."

"They look too good to be true."

"They're good, all right. They're also true."

He grinned shrewdly. "How can I be sure of that?"

"You don't have to take my word for it."

"Oh?"

"See for yourself," she said.

His hand was damp. His fingers trembled as he reached for the redhead. She didn't move. His hand fastened on her breast, cupped it, felt its weight and firmness and softness. His eyes were on hers as he fondled her. Her green eyes looked as though they were swimming in smoke. Her jaw was slack, and she began to breathe hard. He played with her. She wasn't wearing a bra, and he could feel the little button of a nipple go stubbornly stiff against the palm of his hand.

This was no frigid bitch, he thought. Not this one. This gal was nothing like the wife he had left in his room, perfect to look at but useless if you wanted to do more than look. This was a live one, with a short fuse, a girl who got hot as a stove when you ran a hand over her.

And she was built for action, too. The wave of desire that Sue had ignited was powerful now, undeniable in its intensity. He had an urge to throw her down and mount her right there in the middle of the cocktail lounge. Let the whole world watch, he thought. He didn't care. He only cared about having this gorgeous hunk of woman flat on her back with her pretty knees pointing at the sky, and with Mel Dalton between them, stoking her furnace to the hilt with his red-hot poker.

And he guessed that she wouldn't mind a bit. She wouldn't care where they did it or who watched.

Just so they did it.

"I don't know your name," she said suddenly. Her voice was husky, as though she was trying to talk through a cloud of lust.

"Mel."

"I'm Mona."

Mona. Even her name was sexy.

"Mel, I don't want this drink."

"Neither do I."

"Because I don't really feel like drinking."

"Neither do I."

"There's something else I'd rather do. Do you know what I'm talking about, Mel?"

Her hand was on his knee now. She was rubbing him, stroking him, and her hand crawled north until it was inches from the heart and soul of his urgent male passion. Her hand moved higher still and he gritted his teeth and tried to keep from screaming out his lust to the heavens.

"I have a place, Mel."

"Where?"

"Here."

"Here? At the Banzai?"

"Uh-huh."

"Here?"

She smiled lazily. "Sure, honey," she said. "Fifth floor, with a view of the ocean and a big double bed to romp in. A real playground. And do you know something, Mel? We don't have to draw the shades. Nobody can see in, except maybe the fishes. We can just do it and do it and do it—"

"Let's go," he managed to say.

"You sound as though you're in a hurry, Mel." Her hand moved higher and found the object of its search. "Oooooh," she said happily. "I see why you're in a hurry. You're all ready, aren't you, Mel? Well, we can't let that go to waste, can we?"

He couldn't speak. The hot little bitch was driving him out of his mind.

"Come on," she murmured. "Let's hurry, and then you can put your pride and joy to use and we'll have a wonderful time."

Now they were in her room, a room very much like the one he and Sue shared. They were in her room. The door was shut and the window was open, and he was reaching for her. But she dodged away from him, giggling, and he stumbled forward foolishly and sprawled on the bed.

"Not that way, Mel," she said. "You don't want to muss my dress, do you?"

Muss it? He wanted to rip it off of her.

"Let me do a little dance for you. Would you like that? I was going to be a stripper once, Mel, but I decided not to. I only like to show it to one man at a time, not a whole crowd. Besides, it must be awfully frustrating, don't you think? Imagine a girl taking off all of her clothes on stage, and having all of those men staring at her and wanting her and calling dirty things to her. Then when her act is finished she's all hot and bothered and can't do a thing about it. If I were a stripper I don't think I could stand it. I'd have to have a man waiting in my dressing room to take care of me the minute I finished my act."

She moved away from him. He stayed on the bed and watched her. She danced around the room, moving her hips in a swaying shuffle that spoke volumes of unprintable words to him. Her hands went behind her back and played with the zipper on her dress. She opened the zipper all the way and let the dress begin to slip from her shoulders. Mel caught a delicious glimpse of her breasts before she giggled like a schoolgirl and pulled the dress back in place. She let it fall forward once again, almost exposing her nipples, and once again she pulled it back in place.

He wanted to lunge for her, to grab her and slam it to her. But he held himself in check. He knew that it would be better the longer he had to wait for it. When he finally got to her, she was going to be hell on wheels. It would be worth it to wait. And the little show she was putting on was a hell of a performance. If she were ever to become a stripper, he thought, she would have men racing up onto the stage to rape her. They'd have to give her a guard to keep her safe.

And the guard would probably rape her, as far as that went.

Now she shrugged her creamy shoulders once more, and this time the dress fell forward and she did not attempt to catch it. It bunched up around her ankles and she stepped out of it neatly and kicked it across the room.

She was magnificent.

A goddess.

A beauty.

Her breasts were huge, larger even than he had realized at the bar downstairs. He had held one of them, had toyed with it, but even so he had not realized just how perfectly she was built. Her breasts were two cone-shaped cannon shells, flawless mounds of ivory flesh tipped with two pink rosebud nipples. The nipples were surging with passion, stiff and proud. The breasts jutted out from her chest with not the slightest tell-tale trace of sag. They were perfect, breasts as breasts should be.

Mel's mouth watered. He leaned forward, got up from the bed. She laughed at him. He lunged for her, and she ducked away from him and scooted around to the other side of the bed.

No slip, no girdle, no bra. Just a garter belt and stockings and high-heeled black pumps. Her feet were not so small as Sue's, he saw, but they were lovely and well-formed.

"I don't wear panties," she cooed now. "It makes me feel too confined to wear them. I like to be able to breathe down there."

What a girl!

"Mel? Would you like to take my shoes off?"

He nodded, unable to speak now. She came over to the side of the bed. He sat down on the bed. She lifted one leg and put her foot into his hands. His eyes followed her leg all the way up to the top. He thought his chest would burst from the furious pounding of his heart. She was a real redhead, he saw. And a beautiful one.

He held her little foot in his hands. His fingers stroked the smooth black leather as tenderly as if he were stroking the secret parts of her perfect body. He pressed his cheek against her shoe, then raised it to his lips and kissed it. He kissed the dagger-like spike heel, the sole, the toe.

Then, his hands trembling insanely, he took the shoe off.

And kissed her foot through the stocking.

"Mmmmm," she purred. "I like that."

He let go of her foot. She stood on it and presented him with the other foot. His hands once again stroked smooth leather, stroked tenderly. His lips kissed. Finally, he took off the second shoe as well and pressed his mouth against her foot.

When she withdrew her foot, finally, he was shaking like a leaf. She told him to get undressed. He managed to stand up and tore off all of his clothing in a furious hurry. He ripped off his shirt, unzipped his pants and kicked them off. He peeled off every stitch of clothing and stood naked in front of her. He could feel her eyes on him.

She liked what she saw.

"You're a big man, Mel."

He could barely breathe.

"A real big man," she said. She made an O of her mouth and ran her tongue teasingly around her lips. "I love big men," she told him. "I'm crazy about them."

He reached for her. Again, she teased him by ducking away from him.

"Should I leave my stockings on, Mel?"

He nodded.

"Some men like it when I leave my stockings on. They like the way it feels against their thighs and everything. But I'll take them off if you want me to. It's up to you, Mel. Should I take them off or leave them on?"

"Leave them on."

"I was hoping you'd say that," she said.

And then she threw herself onto the bed.

It was hard for him to hold himself in check, but he knew he had to make it last as long as he could. The longer it lasted the better it would be. With Sue, he always tried to finish as soon as possible. She didn't enjoy it, and so he couldn't enjoy it either, so he only tried to get it over with as soon as possible, to take the sweet spurt of release as soon as it would come.

With Mona, he knew how good it would be.

And he damn well wanted to make it last.

He joined her on the bed. She sighed and rolled into his arms. He felt her mountainous breasts against his chest, burning two holes into his flesh. Her arms wound around his neck like a pair of hungry snakes. Her mouth met his, and they kissed. She was a woman who knew what kissing was all about. Her lips parted at once, and her fiery pink tongue darted out and entered his mouth. She kissed him expertly. Her tongue moved cleverly within his mouth, teaching him new delights, lighting little fires wherever it touched. He let his lips close around her tongue and he sucked on it hard, sucked it as though he wanted to tear it out by the roots. Her little gasp of pleasure told him that she liked to be kissed that way.

There were lots of ways to kiss her. Sooner or later he wanted to try them all.

But now his hands moved to her breasts. She let him catch hold of them, and when he began to manipulate the giant orbs of warm flesh she went out of her mind. He had gotten to her this way before, in the bar. But now there was no cloth to separate her flesh from his hands and now he could really give her a good working over. He pinched her nipples and felt them get stiffer and harder than ever. He cupped her breasts and squeezed, and her lips parted and her eyes closed and she moaned and thrashed like a hot little animal in heat, going crazy from his caresses.

He moved on the bed, hungry for her, hungry to taste the sweetness of her delicious breast flesh. She was wiggling her hips and panting, begging him to go ahead and do it to her, but now he wanted to make her wait for it. He found her breast with his mouth and he began to drive her out of her mind.

His tongue coursed over her breast, teasing her, making little circles around the turgid nipple. The circles grew smaller and smaller and he came closer and closer to the hot little rosebud at the tip of that perfect breast, closer and closer and closer, until at long last he found the nipple with his tongue and pressed it like a doorbell, pressed it hard with his tongue.

She moaned.

He caught the nipple between his lips and worked on it, kissing her with all the furious passion that raged within his system, kissing her and sucking at her. His hands did not remain still. He ran a hand up along her stockinged leg and past the top of the stocking. He found her and she was moist and ready and warm.

He flitted from one breast to the other and back again, back and forth, lashing her into a state of raging desire. Her legs were wide apart and her feet were beating out an urgent tattoo at the foot of the bed. Her hips were bucking, tossing up and down and back and forth. She was making wild movements, itching for it, aching for it, asking for it.

"Now," she begged him. "Now, now, now!"

But he made her wait. His urgent manhood was stiff with lust, demanding relief, but he forced himself to wait, too. He caressed her more, more, and she was screaming his name, shouting for him to hurry, begging him to do it.

It was time.

With a choked sob, he threw himself upon her and surged into her warm wet flesh.

It was wild.

Wild?

It was more than that. It was hot and wild and fast and furious and mad. It was the whole world on fire, caught up and flaming, burning with a bright blue flame. It was Mel and Mona playing Adam and Eve. It was the jungle, with drums beating rhythmically in the distance and the palm trees swaying and the natives dancing and the heat of their passion unbelievable.

It was great.

He moved slowly at first, after the initial thrust into her lush embrace. His chest was tight upon her breasts, and her legs had twined around his body like a vine around the trunk of a tree, holding him snug in his place. And, slowly, he began to move within her. With long, low, slow strokes he moved into her and away from her, stirring her deeply, letting the fires build up deep within the confines of her secret flesh.

Slowly.

Then faster—

Faster—

Faster—

Until he was pounding at her at breakneck speed, surging into her, powering his furious maleness in and out of that spiderweb of silky lust. He felt her stockinged legs rubbing furiously against his body, and he felt the insistent pressure of her breasts, and her arms tight around him, and her nails digging into his back, adding a touch of pain that only increased his pleasure.

Faster.

Faster.

It had never been like this before for him. He had had other women, plenty of them. He had had women whom he had paid for, he had had women who gave it for free. He had had his wife, and he had had other men's wives, and he had had whores and tramps and every kind of woman on earth.

But he had never had anything like Mona.

Never before had he met a woman who could pitch his passion so high. Never before had he met a woman who could meet his hunger with equal desire of her own. Never before had he met a woman who could do so much so well.

She was the end of the world. She was what the songs were about, what the whole business of life was about. Maybe she was a tramp, a slut. Maybe she was no good for anything but bedroom games. He didn't care, didn't give a damn. She was what he wanted now, and he was having her, and nothing else mattered at all.

Nothing.

Nothing on earth.

Their bodies were swimming in sweat and the room

reeked with the acrid odor of lovemaking. Faster and faster their bodies moved, hips pounding pleasure into hips, the insistent ragged rhythm of their love spurring them to greater and greater heights. He felt as though he couldn't hold back a second longer, but he forced himself, held himself in check, and then—

Then it began.

He felt her body heave and gasp and spurt and buckle and sway and split and soar. He felt it as wave after wave of crazy passion shot its course through her screaming flesh, felt it as she went into undulant spasms of silken lust. She cried out, a shrill shriek that cut the world in half. She broke apart with passion, and then, as she hovered at the delirious crest of it, his hunger spat forth in a burst of flame and he reached the crisis with her.

The whole world fell apart. The sky came down and the sun went out and the moon turned black. The stars winked and died.

And, gasping, he sprawled upon her naked body and let the blackness fall upon him like a cloud.

"SON OF A GUN," she said.

He rolled over and looked at her. He felt better than he had ever felt in his life. His flesh ached but he didn't mind the ache at all. On the contrary, it felt damned good.

"You're the best," she said.

"You're not so bad yourself."

"I thought I was going to die there, for awhile. I thought the earth was going to open up and swallow me whole, and to tell you the truth I wouldn't have minded it a bit. You're the greatest, Mel. You know how to make a girl go crazy."

He didn't say anything. What a dynamo she was, he thought. And what a piece of luck to find her. A piece of luck to find a piece of tail, he thought. And he smiled at the thought.

"How do you feel, Mel?"

"I never felt better."

"How long will you be in Miami?"

"A couple of weeks."

"So will I. You're from New York, aren't you? I'm from Philly. That's not too far from New York."

"Not far at all."

"We can probably get together after our vacation too, if you want."

"I want," he said.

"So do I. Are you married, Mel?"

He started to say that he wasn't, then changed his mind. A girl who would go the way this one would go wouldn't give a damn if he was married or not. He told her he was married.

"Is your wife in New York?"

"No, I brought her along."

"Brought her along to cheat on her?"

He grinned. "Sue's a good-looking bitch, but she's as cold as a chunk of ice. She doesn't like sex. I brought her along on this trip, but that doesn't mean I plan to spend much time with her."

"I don't blame you." She sighed lazily. "I love to make love," she said.

"I figured that much out for myself."

"I really love it. I can never get enough. I suppose that makes me a nymphomaniac, but I have too much fun to care what it makes me. Just so somebody makes me."

He reached out a hand and touched her.

"I'm in the mood," she said, very softly. "I could go another round, Mel. If you feel up to it."

He felt up to it.

Chapter Four

SUE DALTON LAY ON her back with her eyes closed. She was completely naked. The bedclothing had been turned down so that she was lying nude on the sheet. She could hear the rustle of fabric as Kay took off her clothes. With an effort she opened her eyes and looked at the older woman.

Beautiful, she thought.

Simply beautiful.

She looked at Kay's thighs, at her legs, at her slightly rounded belly. She looked at Kay's breasts and felt a wave of passion at the sight that threatened to overcome her. Kay turned around to hang her bra over a chair, and she looked at Kay's rounded buttocks and her mouth began to water.

Then, with an effort, she closed her eyes once more and forced herself to relax. This was the best way to make love as far as she was concerned. To lie utterly relaxed with her eyes closed while a woman made love to her. She preferred it that way. She liked to be completely passive, to receive caresses without doing anything in return, without even making her response obvious. She would lie like a mummy, receiving everything bestowed upon her, until it all built up to a climax that thrilled her in every fiber of her being. That was the best way, and she loved it.

Of course, she would do more than that later on. After the first flush of warmth, after the first bursting of the dam, after the first tidal wave of fiery lust, she would participate wholeheartedly, her caresses running the whole gamut of lesbian lovemaking. But at the onset she preferred to remain completely passive. She would lie still, inert, motionless, and Kay, her Kay, would do all the work for the time being.

"Susan."

She heard her name spoken. She made no response.

"I want you, Susan."

She waited.

"I'm going to be very good to you, you little darling. I'm going to make you so happy you won't believe it. I know a million tricks, darling. Tricks no man could think of in a thousand years. I know ways to drive a woman insane. It takes a woman to make proper love to a woman, Susan."

That was true, and she knew it. Men wanted to get into you and hurt you and root around in you and dump their passion into you as if you were a wastebasket. Women alone knew how a woman was to be loved. There was no comparing the two forms of sex. With a man it was something to be endured when you had no choice, something to be avoided if you could possibly manage to find a way to avoid it, something to be postponed until the last minute and, when there was no way out, to be carried out and concluded as quickly as possible.

But with a woman it was entirely different. With a woman it was slow and lingering and beautiful. With a woman there was no invasion, no penetration, nothing but a gradual build-up of tender and gentle caresses that got better and better and better as one was piled on top of another, caresses that pitched your feverish passion higher and higher as they went along until your whole body glowed and your soul sprouted wings and flew, until you reached that little bit of Nirvana and saw the face of time.

With a man it was hell. With a woman it was heaven.

And she knew it.

The bedsprings sighed softly as Kay joined her upon the bed. She could feel the warmth of Kay's succulent flesh, near her but not yet touching her. She breathed easily, waiting, waiting for it to begin.

It began.

"Just lie very still," she heard Kay saying to her. "Just lie very still and let me love you."

She did just that.

And Kay began.

First she felt lips on her lips, soft lips, the soft, sweet, good-tasting warmth of a woman's mouth on her own mouth. Kay's tongue flicked out and coursed gently over Sue's closed lips, tasting them, warming them. Kay went on kissing her mouth, not yet touching her with her hands, and Sue lay still and enjoyed it.

Then Kay's mouth left her mouth and Kay's lips traveled along the side of her face, leaving a trail of tiny gentle kisses in their wake. She felt Kay's lips brushing against the nape of her neck, then nuzzling her ear.

Then Kay's whisper, low and intense. "You're going to love everything I do to you, girl. You're going to ache all over and love it. You're going to feel things you never felt before. You're going to love me, Susan."

Kay began to kiss her, teasing her ear with her lips and tongue and teeth. She nibbled at Sue's earlobe. Her tongue darted deep into Sue's ear. It felt funny, and it also felt mysteriously exciting. Sue lay still and enjoyed this as she had enjoyed the kisses on her lips. She let her mind unwind entirely.

She began to remember the first few times, the first times with women. She was just married then, and she was sick inside, sick because she hated what Mel did to her every chance he got. She didn't like it with him, and she knew that there must be something wrong with her. A wife was supposed to love it when her husband did it to her. But how could any woman enjoy that sort of thing?

She couldn't understand it herself. Some women might want it, might actually love it, but she couldn't figure it out. It was rough and coarse and ugly and distinctly unpleasant when Mel did it to her, and she hated it.

Then she met the woman who lived in the apartment next door. They became friends. They had coffee together in the afternoons. They went to an occasional movie together, visited museums and art galleries. Mel didn't care for art or music, so it was a pleasure for her to have a friend who enjoyed that sort of thing.

Gradually, as they became closer to one another, Sue talked about her sex life. The words came pouring out of her in a torrent. She told her new friend how she felt, how Mel's caresses were repulsive to her. She told her everything, and that was what her friend had been waiting to hear.

They made love that very day.

It was a new world opening up for Sue. Now all at once she knew what all the shouting was about. She found out what sex was and what it could be when it worked the way it was supposed to work. She found out that she was a lesbian, found out the sort of pleasure which she could expect to find in the arms and legs of another woman. She couldn't have this pleasure with Mel, but that did not mean that she was frigid.

It meant that she was a lesbian.

She had a wonderful affair with her neighbor. For months they were together every chance they got, which was often. Every afternoon they were in the neighbor's bed, making wonderful love that jolted Sue clear down to the tips of her toes.

Then the neighbor left town.

And then she had to go out to gay bars if she wanted to find someone to have sex with. Her sex life was cut down to the bone. She was frustrated all the time, horny all the time, and there was nothing she dared to do about it.

Maybe she should have left Mel. She had thought about it often enough. She certainly didn't love him. But he was a meal ticket, and that had to count for something. Sooner or later, back in New York, she would have to find a way to get her sex on a steady basis without sneaking around to bars. One lover, say, who could come to her every afternoon in her apartment. That would make it perfect. She would have the money and the status and the comfort that went with being Mrs. Melvin Dalton, and she would have the pleasure that she could get only with another woman.

Her eyes were closed, her breathing shallow.

And Kay's lips made her stop thinking.

KAY WAS KISSING HER breasts now. Sue's breasts were

magnificent, and enormously sensitive. When Mel touched her, grabbing her the way he had grabbed her recently, it made her almost physically ill. She got sick to her stomach and wanted to turn around and run and hide from him.

But when a woman touched her, it was different.

Completely different.

Entirely different.

Kay was curled up on the bed beside her. With soft gentle fingers she was stroking Sue's full breasts, teasing them awake, playing with them. She rolled Sue's nipples between her thumbs and forefingers, rolled the pink buttons to and fro, pulled on them, poked at them. Her fingers moved and her hands filled themselves with Sue's big breasts. She flexed Sue's flesh rhythmically, squeezing, relaxing, squeezing, relaxing—

Then her lips joined the game.

She began by kissing Sue's throat. Then her mouth moved lingeringly downward. Her tongue darted out to flick at silky skin. Lower and lower Kay's mouth moved, coming tantalizingly close to Sue's big breasts. Sue felt as though she were being given a bath, as though she were being bathed by a human tongue. Kay was washing her, washing away all the aches and pains of frustration, leaving only the mellow glow of deliciously forbidden desire.

Closer.

Closer—

And then Kay was busy with her breasts, kissing them, her mouth doing unimaginably delightful things to Sue. She licked the underside of each breast where the skin was soft beyond belief. She washed each breast in turn with the tip of her velvety tongue.

She kissed them.

She sucked them.

FIRES WERE RAGING WITHIN Sue's body, but you would never have known this to look at her. Even now she lay as still as a corpse upon the bed. She did not move, and even her face was calm, with no signs of the tension of sexual excitement. Some girls didn't like it when she lay like this, she knew. Some girls wanted the obvious signs of sexual and sensual response. Otherwise, they didn't think Sue enjoyed it, and this watered down their own pleasure.

But Kay didn't seem to mind.

And Sue, for her part, was burning up inside. Each touch of Kay's miraculous mouth sent new shivers of delight coursing through her warm flesh. Each new caress piled upon the ones that had preceded it, bringing more pleasure and more warmth and more desire in its wake. Every moment was a new source of delight, and she knew now that this would be the best little session of loving she had had in ages. Maybe the best ever.

Kay moved once more on the bed, moved upward this time. Kay's lips touched Sue's lips, and Kay was kissing her, only now Kay had changed her position on the bed so that her whole body was suspended directly above Sue's body.

She lowered herself slightly.

Her breasts moved downward to touch Sue's breasts.

And this was a new delight, a marvelous delight. Slowly, gently, Kay began to move the upper part of her body from side to side, this way and that way. The tips of her own breasts brushed back and forth across Sue's hard nipples. Back and forth, back and forth, with the urgent delight of the breast contact added to the delicious taste of Kay's mouth on her own mouth. Back and forth, and her breasts ached and throbbed from the contact, and her legs opened, and now Kay lay full length upon her so that two pairs of breasts were pressed tight together. And Kay's belly was pressed to her belly, and Kay's legs touched her legs, and Kay's hot fiery loins were pressed tight against the heartland of Sue's enormous hunger.

Kay's body moved.

And moved.

And moved.

The whole process was deliriously effective. Sue had trouble remaining still. She wanted to squirm under Kay, wanted to increase the wonderful feelings that inflamed her. They were pressed taut against one another from head to toe, mouths glued in a divine kiss, breasts giving pleasure to breasts, legs locked in holy combat, loins throbbing against loins. The contact, the pressure, the friction—all of this was utterly delightful.

And Kay was speaking now, her voice pitched lower than ever, lower than a man's voice.

"You little darling. Oh, you baby, you doll. What a body you have. I'd like to eat you up, baby. You kitten, you angel, I could eat you with a spoon."

Her head swam. She was on fire, a pillar of fire like Lot's wife in the daytime. She glowed and burned with lust. She was insane, mad with passion, wild with desire.

"Sue, Sue, Sue. What a body you've got. Your breasts, your legs, your mouth, your everything. I'm going to make you see the stars, girl. Oh, what I'm going to do to you!"

And all the while their bodies were locked together, moving together, and Sue felt passion rising to heights she had not believed existed. And even so she knew that all of this was just the beginning, that it would go on for a long time yet. They would make it last forever, and when the finale came, when it all ended, it would end with an explosion that would register on seismographs in Hong Kong. It would be the start of the greatest earthquake in history. It would split the whole damned world in half.

"Sue, Sue, Sue—"

Slowly, slowly, Kay's body slipped away from her. Slowly, slowly, Kay moved downward, downward, stopping only for a moment to plant new kisses on Sue's breasts, then moving once more inexorably downward to the object of her search.

"What legs. What perfect legs."

And she began to kiss Sue's legs, nibbling at them, licking at them, working her way upward.

Now it was almost impossible for Sue to remain still. She fought against the urges to move, to thrash around. And her desires shifted gears the way she wanted them to. The passion increased with every moment, but her body stayed as motionless as ever. All the hunger was bottled up within her. None of it expressed itself through movement of any sort.

Kay's hungry mouth came closer.

Closer.

And then, magnificently, Sue was the flower in the field, and Kay was a busy bee, draining every last drop of her precious nectar.

IT TOOK A LONG time for the world to come back to normal. It took a long time for the first bright edge of the glow to wear off. There was a long stretch of time during which she lost consciousness, blacking out completely from the force of her climax. When at last she came to again she could not move at first. It was as though every muscle in her body was incapable of motion. Finally, with a tremendous effort, she rolled over on her side and opened her eyes.

Kay was sitting on the edge of the bed, still nicely naked, looking down at her with happy eyes.

"How do you feel?"

"Divine."

"How do you manage to stay still like that? If I didn't know better I would have thought you weren't getting anything out of it. But I could tell that you loved every minute of it."

"That's putting it mildly."

"But how did you stay so passive?"

"I don't know. I like to do it that way. Do you mind?"

"Not at all."

"Are you sure?"

"I'm very sure. I had a good time, Sue."

"I hoped you would."

"I did."

She yawned lazily. "What time is it?"

Kay told her.

"I should get back to the room soon," she said. "I've got a husband who might come around looking for me. But I'll tell you the truth. I don't really give a damn if he looks for me or not. And I just don't feel like leaving you now."

"Good."

"I want to stay here for a long time."

"I want you to."

"All night, even. If we get hungry we can always send down to room service for food."

"If we get hungry," Kay said meaningfully. "We don't have to do that, Sue."

"Oh?"

"We've got each other."

Sue laughed happily. Oh, this was going to be one hell of an afternoon, she thought. One perfect beauty of an afternoon. She had Kay, and Kay was all she needed. The two of them could taste every forbidden pleasure, could pile one bout of love upon another until the world stood on end and winked at them.

Just thinking about it made her get all horny all over again. It was amazing. All she had to do was think about it and she started to itch. And she wouldn't want to be passive this time. This time she would be ready to play the game all the way.

All the way.

No holds barred.

"Where do you live, Kay?"

"Anywhere."

"Huh?"

"I get a steady income from my uncle's estate," the older woman explained. "I'm not crazy rich, but I'm pretty comfortable."

"Damned right you are."

"I mean financially."

"I meant physically."

"I know what you meant. But I have a regular income, and it means I don't have to work for a living. So naturally there's no real reason for me to stay in one place. I go wherever I want to go and do whatever I want to do. I've been down here for a little over a month now. Sooner or later, I'll get tired of this place and go somewhere else. I don't know where I'll go next, or when."

"I hope you won't be leaving too soon."

"How long will you be in Miami, Sue?"

"A couple of weeks."

"I'll stay as long as you do."

"Good."

"And then I'll go somewhere. I don't know where, and it's not worth thinking about it for the time being. Because we've got better things to do than think, don't we?"

"Yes."

Kay reached out a hand and touched Sue's breast. She played with the nipple and smiled as it stiffened. Sue began to squirm. Her breathing went ragged and her hips slipped into the timeless motions of lust.

"You're not so passive now, are you?"

"Not now."

"Quite a change."

"Oh, I get pretty active when I warm up."

"Do you?"

"Uh-huh."

"And then what happens, Sue?"

"Then everything happens."

"Really?"

"Really."

"That sounds interesting," Kay said. "A lot of girls have a few things that they don't like to do. They draw the line somewhere. Are you like that?"

"Not me."

"Honestly?"

"Honestly."

"Will you do what I just did for you?"

"Of course." Sue licked her lips and grinned. "After all," she said, "turnabout is fair play."

"And you like to play fair?"

"I love to play fair."

"That's good to know," Kay said.

And all at once they both started to laugh. Kay threw herself down on the bed and they were in each other's arms in an instant, their hungry mouths joined in a kiss. Their tongues met and became well acquainted. Their breasts rubbed together like old friends, and their legs played games, and they gave themselves over to the delights of the embrace.

"You kiss very well, Sue."

"Just wait. I'll kiss you better than this."

"Will you?"

"I said I would, didn't I?"

"So you did."

How good this was, Sue thought. Not like with a man, not like that at all. So lazy, so dreamy, so utterly beautiful in every respect. She had meant what she had said to Kay. There was nothing she would not do for another woman. The girls she had known in New York had taught her many tricks—things they liked to do, things they liked to have done to them. She enjoyed everything, all of it, top to bottom, inside and out. She was game for anything.

There was a time when she had not been like this. There was a time when she had enjoyed receiving the more intimate caresses of lesbian love but had been unwilling to bestow those caresses in return. She had tried to draw a line, doing certain things and refusing to do other things.

Gradually her neighbor had changed her attitude. Little by little she learned that there could be no holds barred in love, that anything went. Little by little she learned that there was as much pleasure in giving as there was in receiving. Little by little she learned what to do and how to do it.

Now, her hands on Kay's breasts, she smiled the smile of a girl who knew and a girl who put her knowledge to work.

"It's my turn," she murmured.

And she moved downward on the bed, ready now, ready to do what Kay had done.

She was ready.

And she was hungry.

Chapter Five

When Mel Dalton got dressed and left her room, Mona stayed in bed for half an hour, her head on her pillow, her eyes closed. She was not sleeping, merely resting. She smiled a private smile from time to time. Then, lazily, she stretched her arms high overhead, yawned lustily, and swung her legs over the side of the bed. She stood up, then dropped to one knee and reached under the bed. She withdrew a portable tape recorder powered by transistors. She turned it off and took the two-hour reel of tape from the spindle. In one of her dresser drawers she found a small cardboard box. She fitted the reel of tape in the box and marked the box *Melvin Dalton—1* in red ink. Then, still grinning, she locked the reel away in a metal strongbox which she kept on the top shelf of the closet.

The tape, she knew, would require careful editing. Whole stretches of it were filled up with nothing but the monotonous if provocative sound of creaking bedsprings—fun to play at parties, no doubt, and geared to bring back fond memories, to be sure, but hardly likely to be too effective an instrument for blackmail.

An instrument for blackmail. She sat on the edge of

the bed and gazed downward fondly at the triangle of red hair below her belly. That's what you are, she told the area. You're just a sweet little instrument for blackmail.

But the tape could be edited easily enough, she knew. There was plenty of conversation in between the snatches of sexy silence. Conversation that would nail one Mel Dalton to the wall. Conversations wherein he told her just what he liked to do, and how much he hated his iceberg wife, and how good Mona was in the hay, and so on and so forth ad infinitum. And, if you were not made of sterner stuff, occasionally ad nauseam.

Mona yawned and stretched again. There was always the possibility that she would never use the tape, of course. She didn't blackmail every man who shared her bed. If she did, she'd be the richest woman on earth, because her bed was rarely empty. A truly promiscuous nympho, she had found a way to make her hobby pay off without being so crude as to set up shop as a full-fledged prostitute.

The idea of putting out for money did not appeal to Mona in the least. She wanted to enjoy her sex all the way, and money in return for services rendered would only spoil her fun. But afterward, when the man had left her, when he had nearly forgotten her—well, that was a different story. Then it was simple to make him pay a big pile of money in return for a reel or two of tape. Or let him pay a little at a time—say a hundred dollars a month, forever.

Sometimes it was better to hit a victim for a big chunk of cash all at once, then give him the tape and get out of his life. With other men, it was better to let them put her on the payroll. She was smarter than most blackmailers in that she knew enough to be satisfied with no more than the man could easily pay. If she asked for too much too often, a victim might be tempted to take the easy way out by arranging to have Little Miss Mona killed as dead as a week-old herring. But as long as she kept the bite small, she didn't have any worries on that score.

And she made a decent (or indecent, depending upon your point of view) living out of it. A hundred a month was no fortune, certainly. But when you had fifteen or twenty guys each kicking in with a hundred a month, and when you had an occasional one-shot score for three or four grand, then it added up pretty neatly.

She always picked her victims carefully. If a man showed her a very good time in the sack, an unusually good time, say, then she was more likely to let him off the hook. Otherwise, she would pick men who could afford to pay off and who had good reason to do so. Men who wanted to keep their marriages intact, for example. Men who had a position in the community would be shot to hell by a tape recording like the ones she made. Men who couldn't afford to let the world know the odd ways they got their kicks.

It paid off.

It paid off in a fairly big way. But she wasn't greedy. She wanted enough money so that she could buy whatever clothes she wanted, go wherever she wanted, live as well as she wanted, and sock a little dough in the bank for a rainy day. That was all. And she had no trouble getting everything she wanted.

In the beginning she had had a partner. Her partner was a thin-faced hollow-eyed little man named Willie Retch, a squeaky-voiced son of a gun who was an absolute genius with a camera. He knew how to shoot with infra-red flashbulbs that made no light and that could take pictures in utter darkness. He could hover silently in a closet, waiting instinctively for just the right moment to open up his hand-made peephole and zoom in on the action unfolding before him. Willie had taken good pictures and she had provided good action, and they had split proceeds down the middle.

It had been fun at first. The pictures were pretty interesting, and it was exciting to look at photographs of yourself making love afterward.

But there were things that bothered her about the arrangement. For one thing, she wasn't too crazy about the idea of somebody else watching while she was getting her jollies. That could be a kick now and then, but after awhile she got to feeling like a performer, and that was no fun at all. It made her self-conscious. There were times when she had trouble getting into the spirit of the sex act because of it, and that was bad.

And she knew that Willie got a kick out of watching.

But the most important reason why she didn't like the set-up was that she got to the point where she couldn't stand Willie Retch at all. He was an utterly unappealing little man with a twisted mind and strange tastes. At first she hadn't minded so much, because she was the sort of girl who always appreciated novelty as far as sex was concerned.

Still, the novelty had to wear off sooner or later.

Willie's kick had been a complicated rigamarole, she remembered. The little punk was bizarre when it came to dressing up in her clothes. He'd deck himself out in her wildest stuff—flimsy lingerie, tight girdles that she never bothered with, bras that were fairly absurd on his breastless body, and strapless gowns with plunging necklines. Then he would stuff his scrawny legs into a pair of her nylons, wedge his flat feet into a pair of her high heels, and spend an hour or so primping in front of her mirror, piling on the eye shadow and the mascara and the lipstick and dabbing himself with perfume until he reeked like a Parisian madame.

That was bad enough, and she thought rather seriously that if Willie Retch was that crazy about turning himself into a woman he ought to take the next plane to Denmark and get his equipment altered. But he didn't want to, evidently.

What he wanted was to come on like that, dressed up more like a girl than most girls, and kneel on the floor in front of her while she beat his behind with a leather strap. She never hit him very hard because she was afraid she'd do some real damage. But he would cower there, babbling that she was his mistress and he was her slave, and she would be all dressed up in a fur coat with nothing under it, and she would pound away at him while he went on like that.

Then, finally, they would try to make it together. It was enough of a drag what with him stinking of perfume and cosmetics, and it was even more of a drag in that Willie Retch was a real rabbit, an on-again-off-again thirty-second man. He was through before she even got started, and if there was one thing she couldn't stand it was a man who got off halfway through the ride.

So, she did the only logical thing under those particular circumstances. She replaced Willie Retch with a tape recorder.

It was a good exchange. The tape recorder demanded nothing. She didn't have to find some odd way to ball it. All she had to do was put a reel of tape on, flick the switch, then take the tape off afterward. Her model had large reels that would hold two solid hours of recorded time. She could start the thing before she went out, pick up a man, take him to her room, bang him, get rid of him, and still have time left over. Or, more often, she could get the guy into the bathroom somewhere in the course of things and turn the tape recorder on before he came back.

The tapes weren't as jarring as the pictures. But with the right victim, the quality of the evidence didn't matter much. The simple threat of exposure often did the trick. With the pictures, they had rarely actually been forced to show them to the victim. All she had to do was announce that she had the pictures in her possession, and that generally turned the trick.

She sighed now and headed for the bathroom. She had a nice sexy smell to her body, and in a way it was almost a shame that she had to wash it away. But it just wouldn't do to walk around smelling of one man's lust when she was looking for another man. And of course, she intended to find another man somewhere in the course of the evening. She was born for sex, crazy for sex, and she took whatever came her way. Whenever she found a man in the mood who looked as though he'd be fun in the sack, she went to bed with him. In all her life she had never found a solitary damned thing on earth that was more fun than the pleasure she got from sex. Nothing else could ever equal it.

She turned on the shower, stepped under it. She

washed quickly but thoroughly, lathering herself from head to toe with her special brand of perfumed soap, then rinsing herself completely, soaping again, rinsing a final time. She stepped nimbly out of the shower and dried herself quickly and thoroughly.

Surveying her nude body in the mirror, she thought how fortunate she had been to be born unusually good looking. Suppose she had been unattractive, she thought.

Then what would she do?

A lot of women could get through life easily enough without being raving beauties. But a woman with Mona's type of sexual appetite had to be damned beautiful if she was going to live the sort of life she craved. She had to be the kind of woman every man ached to score with the minute he set eyes on her. Otherwise, she couldn't get anywhere near as much action as she needed.

And she liked to get as much as she could.

In fact, she could never get too much.

Suddenly she remembered something that had happened just a year ago, in a college town in New England. She had been passing through, and just as a lark she went into one of the local bars and let a college boy buy her a drink or two. When he made his inevitable pass, she was seized with a wicked inspiration.

"Got any friends?" she demanded.

He just looked at her.

"You're a nice kid," she went on, "but I'm going to need more than one lover tonight. How many fellows do you know who'd like a crack at a crack like me?"

At first he took it for granted that she was a prostitute who was looking to take on a whole crowd at five or ten bucks a throw. But she let him know she wasn't interested in making a dime out of the deal, not a red cent.

"I'm just a girl who likes to be loved," she said.

"Just like that?"

"Just like that. Line up a crowd and we'll see who lasts the longest."

He picked an easy way to line up a crowd. He took her back to the fraternity house where he lived, and he smuggled her inside with the ingenuity that does credit to the American system of higher education. He snuck her upstairs and lodged her in a bedroom, and then he called his friends together, and that had turned out to be one perfect dream of a night.

There were twenty-eight boys in the fraternity. Two of them were away for the night, which was their tough luck. Each of the remaining twenty-six took a turn, and nine came back for seconds, and two boys came back for thirds. Which meant, in case you stank in algebra class, that little Mona got her ashes superbly hauled a total of thirty-nine times in the space of a single night.

That, friend, is a lot of sex.

But she weathered it in fine form. She was still going strong when the last boy petered out, and she could have gone a few more rounds with no trouble at all. Still, it had been an utterly satisfying experience. The guys tried hard to get her to stick around for a few days, and she was tempted, but she had a feeling that a few more nights like that one, however enjoyable, might very well kill her or cripple her for life. She had nothing but fond memories of the occasion, however.

Now she got into her clothes—into the few clothes she bothered to wear, that is. She put on a fresh pair of stockings, because Mel Dalton had slobbered over the ones she had worn to bed. She put on a clean garter belt and hooked the stockings to it. She wore the green dress again. It had done well enough with Mel, and it was a good a mantrap as any dress she had. Why kick a proven winner?

A little lipstick, a little perfume. She didn't like to go crazy with makeup. That might come later on in life, when she started to get screwed up with a lot of wrinkles or something. In the meanwhile, she was fine without it.

She checked herself a final time in the mirror, pulling her dress a shade lower to let just a little more of her breasts show. Time for dinner, she thought. She could do one of two things—pick up some man in the cocktail lounge and con him into buying a dinner, or eating by herself and putting it on her hotel tab and picking up a man later on.

She decided on the latter course of action. If she had dinner with a man, she would have to talk and pose all through the meal and would be unable to enjoy her food properly. They would play all those coy games—rubbing knees at the table, loading conversations with double entendres, and all the rest of that nonsense. This could be good clean fun at the proper time, but right now she was hungry. She wanted a meal.

She ate by herself in the hotel restaurant. She sat at a table alone and started off with a bone-dry martini. Then she had a two-inch sirloin, cooked properly rare, with a baked potato loaded with sour cream and a stein of Canadian ale. She had dessert—rhubarb pie a la mode—plus coffee, plus an after-dinner brandy.

No food could have been better and no one could have appreciated it more. That was one thing about sex, she reflected, you really worked up an appetite. She polished off everything, and by the time the meal was over she felt pleasantly stuffed. She drained her brandy glass, signed the check, added a tip, and got to her feet.

It was time to find someone for the night.

Chapter Six

MEL DALTON STIRRED CREAM and sugar into his second cup of coffee. He was in a restaurant called Foxie's, and he had just finished a meal of scrambled eggs and sturgeon, and he felt pleasantly full. He lit a cigarette, sucked in a lungful of smoke, then blew the smoke out and watched it get caught up in the intake of the air-conditioning system. Everything in Miami was air-conditioned, he thought. Everything. One of these days, he told himself, some bright young jerk would put a plastic globe around the whole of southern Florida and air-condition the whole damned place.

It was something to think about.

Not that he was in any great danger of running out of things to think about. After he left Mona's room, he had gone downstairs to his own room to look for his wife. The room had been empty. He waited there, and at seven o'clock she breezed in with a smile on her beautiful face.

"Get dressed," he told her. "We're going to Foxie's for dinner. I'm starving."

"You go ahead," she said.

"Huh?"

"I met a friend while you were gone. A woman named Kay, an old friend."

"You never mentioned her before."

"Didn't I?" Sue shrugged. "Anyway, she's an old friend, and I haven't seen her for ages. She asked me if I'd go with her tonight. There's an art gallery showing some new paintings by an artist who's supposed to be quite excellent. He's an abstract expressionist, Kay says, and his work shows definite influences as far removed as Jackson Pollock and El Greco, and—"

The rest of this was lost on him. As far as Mel was concerned, a picture was a picture. Either you liked it or you didn't, and if you liked it then you stood and looked at it for awhile, and if you didn't like it, then to hell with it. This modern junk, with lines and splats and blotches all the hell over the place—it didn't move him at all. He liked pictures that you could recognize, pictures that said something to you.

Privately, he was convinced that Sue was full of crap as far as art was concerned. He didn't believe she really knew what the hell she was talking about, or that she cared as much for these crazy paintings as she pretended to care. But that was her business. Once in awhile she would make him buy some monstrosity to hang on one of their walls. If it didn't cost more than fifty or a hundred bucks he never gave her an argument. They always looked like hell, and the apartment was getting pretty crapped up with all the garbage she bought, but at least it gave her something to do and kept her quiet. At that price, it was a bargain.

But this didn't mean he liked to look at that kind of garbage. He didn't know much about art, he thought cleverly, but he damn well knew what he liked. As far as he was concerned, a pretty girl with her clothes off was worth all the far-out statues in the world. Talk about art—watching Mona get out of her clothes beat staring at the greatest picture ever painted.

He wondered how one of these abstract expressionist artists would paint a picture of Mona. Probably with arms and legs shooting out of her head, and a blotch of green here and a snatch of red here, and this and that, and the final result would look about as much like the girl he had just finished boffing as the coffee in front of him looked like the Mona Lisa.

No artist could do Mona justice. And she probably couldn't even manage to turn them on. Everybody knew about those bums. They all wore beards and lived like pigs and drank like fish, and every last one of them was a queer.

So, he said, "You really want to go to this thing?"

"Certainly. You're welcome to come with us, if you'd enjoy it."

"Like I'd enjoy hanging."

"You don't have to be so crude, you know."

"Crude," he said. "To hell with this crude crud. I just figured we'd have dinner together the first night in Miami."

"Well, Kay and I—"

"Forget it," he said. "Listen, I think I'll head over to Foxie's then and grab a bite myself. Then maybe I'll take in the jai alai games or go to the dog track. That's a little bit more my speed than looking at pictures."

"To each his own."

"Something like that. You need any money?"

"I have enough."

He dug out his wallet, passed her a fifty. "Here," he said.

"I don't need this."

"Take it anyway."

"I have enough, Mel."

"Maybe you'll see a picture you want to buy. Or a pair of shoes in one of those fancy Lincoln Road shops. It never hurts to have an extra couple of bucks handy, kid."

She didn't give him an argument. He left the room without kissing her good-bye and went downstairs to the lobby.

Actually, he thought, he was secretly relieved to have Sue off his neck for the evening. Another man might have been jealous, but Mel had better things to do than sit around being jealous of a wife like her. That was one thing about being married to an iceberg, he told himself. You didn't have to worry about where she went or who she went with. When she was a frigid bitch to begin with, there was no chance she'd be carrying on with some other man—not when she didn't care for love or sex at all.

And now, with Sue off with her old friend Kay, he had the evening to himself. He stepped out of the air-conditioned lobby into the warm air of the early evening. Maybe, he thought, he should give Mona a call. Maybe he could buy her a dinner—not around the hotel, certainly, but at some decent restaurant somewhere on the Beach.

He slipped back into the lobby, called Mona's room on the house phone. There was no answer. He dropped into the bar on the chance that she might be there, but she wasn't.

Well, the hell with her, he thought savagely. She had been a first-class piece of tail and he intended to get a good sample of her before the trip was over. But if she wasn't around, then the hell with her. He'd make do with scrambled eggs and sturgeon at Foxie's, and after that he'd find some good way to kill the evening.

NOW, AS HE FINISHED his coffee, he tried to figure out something to do for the night. He had told Sue that he might watch the dogs run or drop over to the Fronton for some jai alai action, but that was just something to say to her. Actually, he had been fairly certain that he would wind up spending the night with Mona. But he had just called Mona's room a second time, and this time she had answered with a funny note in her voice, and had told him she was going to sleep early and wouldn't be able to see him.

Going to sleep?

Well, he wasn't about to believe that story, not in a hundred years. She might be going to bed, but she damned well wasn't going to sleep.

And he guessed that she wasn't going to bed alone, either.

He sat at the table now, lit a fresh cigarette from the butt of the old one, closed his eyes tight and gritted his teeth. That was the trouble with getting mixed up with a nympho, he knew. They gave it to everybody. You spent a few hours banging their ears off, and no sooner had you left them than some other ring-tailed cross-eyed, pigeon-brained, fat-headed son of a gun had taken your place between their plump little thighs. You couldn't win with a nympho. She would go like sixty for you, but she would go like sixty for somebody else too. You always wound up feeling as though somewhere along the line you had done something wrong.

The hell with it.

The hell with everything.

Let her take on the whole world, he thought angrily. What the hell did he care? He'd get her whenever he could, and he'd give her a ride she would remember for ages, and that was plenty. In the meantime, he was at least lucky enough to have Sue off his neck.

Why not make the best of it?

He paid his check and left a good tip for the waiter. Then he got out of Foxie's and stood for a moment or two on the pavement outside. The air was still warm, but not so warm as it had been earlier. There was a breeze blowing off the ocean, and the air had a good salt smell to it.

He could go to the dog track. Or he could go to the Fronton. Or he could go back to the hotel and go to sleep.

Sure.

And there was something else he could do. He could go out and find himself another broad.

And that sounded like the best idea of all.

He had an idea where to go. It was still early, he knew, but plenty of nightclubs got going early. And there was one he had heard about, not in Miami Beach but in downtown Miami itself on Flagler. The place was called Nikki's, and it was supposed to swing. He had never been there, but he had heard enough about it to know it was the place he wanted.

An unimpressive place on the surface. They didn't

have plush decor or thick carpets on the floors. And they didn't get the top entertainers, the headliners you could catch at the big Beach hotels. But they had something better than that, according to what Mel had heard. They had the hottest floorshow on earth, and they had enough tail around the joint so that a guy couldn't miss finding something that would appeal to him.

So, what the hell.

How could he lose?

He caught a cab outside of Foxie's. He told the driver where he wanted to go and settled back to enjoy the ride.

"IN A WAY," Kay was saying, "you're a very fortunate woman, Sue."

"Why?"

"Because of your husband."

"My husband? What's fortunate about being married to a pig like Mel?"

Kay shook her head. "If you don't enjoy sex with men anyway, it doesn't make much difference whether you're married to a pig or a Greek God. But that's not what makes you so lucky. The good thing is that he doesn't suspect a thing. Most husbands would be jealous as all get out if their wives ducked away from them the first night of a vacation. Most husbands would think something was funny, a wife running off with her girlfriend every chance she got. But your husband is the most completely trusting man on earth. He must think you don't have any sex at all."

"Maybe that's what he thinks."

"Well, then you're lucky."

"I suppose I am."

"Of course you are."

"Yes. I guess you're right, Kay."

She smiled across the table at the older woman. They were in a small café a few doors down from the hotel on the other side of Collins Avenue away from the ocean front. The café was small, dark and intimate. A slender young man was playing the piano and singing mildly risqué songs. There were several men at the bar. The average person entering the café would never have guessed that it was a homosexual hangout. There were no women in mannish clothing, no men dancing together, no effeminate males, nothing of the sort. The café was as discreet a gay joint as Sue had ever seen. But the fact remained that the clientele was almost exclusively homosexual. The men at the bar were faggots. The tables contained either two males or two females, never a mixed pair. The men were homosexuals and the women were lesbians, and the bar was as gay as a jay and as queer as a square egg.

"Do you like this place, Sue?"

"It's fine."

"I don't generally care for the gay bars. They're noisy and uncouth and far too obvious. When one walks into one of them, one feels immediately that one is meat on a butcher's shelf, waiting for some hungry person to come along and steal you away. I don't like that feeling."

"I know what you mean."

"But this place is pleasant. You're a lovely woman, Sue. I don't see why you stay married at all."

"I've thought about leaving Mel."

"Why haven't you gone ahead with it?"

"I don't know."

"He must be a good meal ticket—"

"He is."

"But that's not enough reason to stay." Kay leaned across the table, took hold of her hand. The older woman's voice was low and intense. "You'd have a much better life on your own, Sue. And you know the way the divorce laws work in this country. You could divorce him and hook him for a healthy chunk of alimony. And—"

"But that doesn't seem fair, does it?"

"Fair?" Kay's eyes mocked her. "What does fair have to do with it? You're not being fair to your husband to begin with. Is it fair of you to be married to him without giving him a sex life? Is it fair of you to cheat on him with women? I'm not blaming you for that, darling. Believe me, I wouldn't blame you for the world. I'm just trying to show you how much better it would be for both of you if you left him. He could take up with some tramp who liked his sort of loving, and you would be free to go where you want and do what you want."

Sue lowered her eyes. There was a lot in what Kay was saying to her and she realized it. Still, she could never quite steel herself to the point where she was prepared to break up her marriage by leaving her husband. It might be the best thing, but that didn't make it easy to take the plunge.

"Sue?"

"What?"

"Have you been listening to me?"

"Of course."

"And do you agree?"

"I suppose so, but—"

The older woman sighed. "Words can only achieve a certain amount," she said. "Words can only do so much convincing, and then something beyond words is called for. I may not be able to talk you into it, darling, but there's another argument I can use."

"Oh?"

"A physical argument."

"You mean—"

"I mean I think we ought to go across the street again," Kay said. "I think we ought to go back to the hotel. Unless you don't feel like it, dear."

"I always feel like it," Sue Dalton said.

Chapter Seven

WHEN THE HOLLOW-EYED man closed the door to her room and turned toward her, Mona realized at once that he had been a mistake. She should never have picked him up. A tape recording of his idea of fun and games would be worthless, in the first place, because for one thing he didn't look as though a blackmail threat could faze him in the least. If you tried to blackmail this sort of man, he would laugh at you and kick your teeth down your throat and then strangle you with your tape.

This in itself didn't matter much. After all, she only blackmailed a fairly miniscule proportion of the men she slept with, and her choice of a bedmate was not predicated upon his possible bank balance nor upon his potential as victim for blackmail. On the contrary, the overwhelming majority of men were chosen simply on the basis of their sexual attractiveness. If Mona thought they might be fun in the hay, she was willing to give them a whirl.

Take the night with the college fraternity, for example. She didn't get a nickel out of that evening's entertainment, and she did more balling than most women did in six months. No, money was not her main consideration. If she thought a man would be fun, she gave him a try.

But this man—

She had a feeling he wouldn't be much fun.

He turned to her now. His eyes burned in his darkly tanned face. When he took off his jacket she could see ridges of hard muscle on his chest, muscles in his shoulders and his arms. He could probably break her in half with no effort at all, she thought. There was something slightly exciting in the thought, but there was also a good deal of terror in it.

She had met this kind before, and she had always thought she was able to recognize them at a glance. The intense stare in their eyes, the aura of barely suppressed violence.

He was that kind.

The rough kind.

The violent kind.

And she was scared.

"Peel," he said.

She looked at him.

"Peel," he said. "Get out of your clothes. Get the dress off, and fast. Get out of everything or you'll wish you did when I told you to."

It was then that the phone had rung. Mel was calling, calling from some place called Foxie's. He wanted to come up and see her. For a hysterical moment she considered telling Mel that a man had her trapped in her room. But what could he do? If she pulled something like that, Bart—that was his name, Bart, and he hadn't told her his last name—Bart would beat the daylights out of her. He would belt her around until she was black and blue, and he would be long gone before Mel got there, or before the police or house detective arrived.

She looked at Bart.

"Get rid of him," she heard him growl.

And so, she got rid of Mel. She fed him some bull about having decided to go to sleep for the night, knowing as she spoke the words that there was not the slightest chance he would believe her. But what else could she do? She cradled the phone and turned to look pleadingly at Bart.

"Now strip," he said.

She knew better than to argue. There were two possible courses of action when you were stuck with a man like Bart. You could try to talk him out of it, either by shaming him or by appealing to his good side or something like that. Or else you could do whatever he asked you to do, and you could do it damned quick without a word of protest. She looked at Bart and she knew how useless it would be to appeal to his good side. If she was any judge at all, it was highly doubtful that he had a good side. He seemed like a thoroughgoing son of a bitch.

So, she went along with him.

Quickly.

And silently.

Without a word she peeled off her dress and tossed it on the chair. She didn't bother putting on a teasing strip the way she had done for Mel. It would have been wasted on Bart. Instead, she took off her clothes with a minimum of excess motion. The dress came off first, leaving her bare entirely except for her garter belt and stockings. She felt his eyes on her breasts and her flesh crawled from the way he was looking at her.

If only she had had the sense to recognize him for what he was at the beginning. If only she had had the brains to guess in advance that he was this type of man. All the signs were present, but somehow she had been too stupid to notice what should have been so very obvious, what had in fact become exceptionally obvious the moment he closed the door.

But by then it was too late. By then she was in the room with him, and there was no way out.

She unfastened her stockings from her garter belt and drew them down to her ankles, kicked off her high heeled shoes, peeled the stockings off and cast them aside. She got out of the garter belt and turned to him wordlessly, naked now, completely naked and defenseless, waiting.

He grinned at her.

It was an awful, leering grin. It sent a shock of fear jetting through every bit of her gorgeous body. She wondered in horror just what he intended to do to her. He could do anything he wanted and there was nothing on earth that she could do about it. He could hurt her. He could mark her flesh. He could even kill her and she had no way out. She was entirely at his mercy.

She decided that she didn't mind a little pain. She could live through it well enough. But she only hoped that he wouldn't mark her up. That would be horrible. Her body and its desirability was her stock in trade, and marks or bruises would be a disaster. If she lived through this, and if she came out of it intact, then everything would be all right. And if nothing else, she would have learned a valuable lesson. She would have learned damn well not to pick up men like Bart.

"Come here, bitch."

He had not removed any of his own clothes. He was standing with his hands on his hips. The muscles worked in his powerful arms. She approached him, stopped a foot away from him.

"Closer."

She drew closer. One of his hands came up to cup her

breast. She cringed under his touch, sure that he was going to tighten his grip on her tender flesh, certain that he would squeeze with all his might until her knees turned to jelly and her eyes filled with tears and she would fall down, crying like a baby.

Instead, he only laughed. He laughed shortly, laughed like a bull snorting in an open field. His hand dropped from her breast and he backed away from her.

"All right," he said. "Get on your knees."

What was he going to do now?

"On your hands and knees. Fast!"

She dropped to her hands and knees.

"Now crawl around the room, you little tramp."

She did what he told her. She began to crawl around the room on her hands and knees. He walked alongside of her and examined every inch of her perfect body from every angle.

"Big breasts," he said.

She kept crawling. She felt dirty now, horribly dirty. She wished he would go ahead and do whatever it was that he intended to do to her, anything just so that he would get it over with. And then she had an awful thought. She had read about girls who were trapped by some sadistic lunatic like Bart, girls who were held captive for days, even weeks. Sometimes these girls would be tortured to the point of death time and time again, saved each time, and always held captive, helpless and defenseless.

Sometimes the girls were dead by the time it was over. And it seemed as though the ones who died were the lucky ones. The others, mutilated in body and mind, wound up living in lunatic asylums, screaming their lungs out and banging their heads against the padded walls, unable to forget for a moment the indignities that these perverts had put them through.

Was this what he had planned for her?

She hoped not.

"Nice rear end," he said.

She kept crawling.

"Good legs."

What did he want from her?

"Get up, you little slut. Up!"

She stood up. He went over to where he had tossed his suit jacket. He picked it up and reached in one of the pockets. A gun, she guessed. Or a knife or a whip or something like that.

But that wasn't what it was.

It was a big yellow banana.

"Here," he said. He tossed the banana to her, and she fumbled it, then managed to catch it. The skin of the yellow fruit was very smooth.

"Peel it."

She peeled the banana. What the hell was this all about? she wondered. It didn't make the slightest bit of sense to her. But she had stopped trying to figure things out. She had decided to do whatever he asked in the hope that she would live through the night.

"You love it, don't you?"

She looked at him.

"Sure, you love it. Now I want you to do some exercises with it, you little slut."

He told her what she was supposed to do with the banana.

And she did everything he asked.

Everything.

And, throughout the entire performance, he merely sat in her chair and watched her put on her act. He sat there while she followed his directions to the letter, sat there and never took his eyes off the performance which she was putting on for him.

Finally, he had had enough. He told her to stop doing what she had been doing, and she stopped. He told her to give him the banana, and she gave it to him.

He gobbled it up in three big bites. Then, with an incredibly weird expression on his darkly handsome face, he turned from her and stalked out of the room. The door slammed hard behind him and she stayed where she was on the floor, eyes wide with shock, heart pounding furiously, breasts heaving spasmodically in fitful time to her heavy ragged breathing.

He was gone.

Gone.

Gone.

It took several minutes for the shock to wear off. Then, when she realized that he was through, that he had gone and would not return, not now and not ever, her terror faded away completely and she began to laugh hysterically, laughing with relief and genuine amusement. She threw back her head and whooped like a hyena with laughing gas. She laughed and laughed, laughed harder than she had ever laughed in her life. She threw back her head and laughed until her cheeks ached and until the tears rolled down her face. She laughed hysterically.

He was a pervert, all right.

And she had finally managed to figure out his particular perversion.

The stupid rotten miserable no-good perverted son of a bitch was queer for bananas.

NIKKI'S WAS AS UNIMPRESSIVE on the surface as Mel Dalton had heard it would be. Dingy, dimly lit, cheap and tawdry, the Flagler Street dive hardly looked like a Mecca for well-heeled tourists. But you couldn't judge everything by appearances. Mel was inside now, sitting at a table down front, drinking a watered-down gin and tonic and smoking a cigarette.

The floorshow was on.

And the floorshow was the reason for Nikki's astonishing commercial success. Already, early as it was, the place was nearly filled. There was a six-dollar-per-person minimum at tables, and drinks were a buck and a quarter per. The place might be a dive, and Nikki might have to pay off a pretty penny in order to operate in the open like this, but there was no question about one thing. The place was a goldmine.

But somehow the floorshow didn't do a thing for Mel. He didn't know why. He didn't want to bother figuring it out, but what the hell, it just wasn't working. The whole deal would cost him fifteen bucks before he was through, and all he was doing was sitting around drinking lousy drinks and watching some broads take their clothes off.

Sure, they went further than broads usually went in strip clubs. They peeled all the way down to the buff, all the way, taking off their pasties and their G-strings, going all the way until they were completely bare.

But so what?

They weren't showing him anything he hadn't seen before.

And he'd seen better ones at that.

Like Mona, for example.

He drew on his cigarette. You could do more than look at Nikki's, he knew. There were plenty of dames around who would take you on for fifteen or twenty bucks, and there were rooms available in the back for a quick tumble. But he didn't want any of the pigs who were hanging around, and he didn't want a quick tumble, either.

He knew what he wanted.

He wanted Mona.

He looked at his watch. It was around nine-thirty now. What time had it been when he called her last? He wasn't sure. Better than an hour ago, at any rate. And maybe she hadn't been with a man, anyway. He had been certain that she was with somebody at the time, but he could have been mistaken. After all, she might have been tired. He had given her plenty to be tired about, he thought, remembering it all with a smile.

The hell with this place, he thought. Let the creeps sit around staring at naked broads and let them carry off the whores to the back rooms.

He was in for something a damned sight better.

He pushed his chair back, got to his feet. He threw money on the table for the drinks and the tip. He pushed his way out of the club, shouldering men out of the way who just moved aside to give him room and then went back to their business of watching girls take their clothes off.

Outside, he hailed a cab. He was on his way back to Mona. The blood lust already pounded in his temples.

Chapter Eight

KAY LAY ON HER side of the bed, eyes closed, breathing slow and even. She was not asleep, however. She knew that Sue was asleep at her side, and for a moment she envied the younger girl. It was good to be able to drift off to sleep after a healthy bout of love making. That was the sweetest kind of sleep that came, the sleep that followed close upon the heels of physical gratification. Nothing could match it. You became excited, and your excitement mounted higher and higher, finally dissolving and exploding in a crystal-clear peak of perfect passion. Then, at once, you moved from excitement to the good clean restorative bliss of sublime sleep.

But Kay couldn't sleep, and she knew she was destined to lie awake for a long time. There was no room for doubt. Her head was as clear as glass, her body totally unprepared for the relaxation that good sleep demanded. And lying in bed would not do her any good at all. Soon she would become restless, and then she would toss and turn, and that was no good at all.

Sometimes there were nights when she could not sleep at all no matter how tired she was. Sometimes there were nights when she tossed and turned for hours on end, finally drifting off into a restless slumber around the time that dawn was breaking in the east, only to wake up a few hours later with a bad taste in her mouth and a burning sensation around her eyes and a deep desire to put the business end of a revolver between her lips and blow a healthy hole in the back of her head. She had never gone this far, obviously, but on days like that she had truly felt in the mood for it.

So, it was foolish to stay in bed now. But she had to be careful not to wake Sue. Accordingly, she slipped noiselessly from the bed, padded barefoot across the carpet to the bathroom where her clothes were hung. She brushed her teeth diligently—a lesbian was well advised to use a mouthwash whenever opportunity permitted, she thought. She washed her hands and face and other parts of her fine body as well, dried herself with a towel, and put on her clothes.

Back in the bedroom, she stopped by the side of the bed and looked down at Sue. Sue was sound asleep, lying sprawled on her back with her hair spread out over the pillow. Her legs were parted, one leg thrust out straight, the other bent deeply at the knee. One of Sue's arms was at the side of her body, the other at a right angle to her body. The girl's mouth was slightly open, her eyes of course shut.

How lovely she is, Kay thought.

There was a pack of cigarettes on the bedside table. Kay picked up the pack, shook a cigarette loose, put it between her full lips. She scratched a match, lit the cigarette and drew down a lungful of smoke. She pursed her lips as if to kiss and blew out a thin column of smoke that hung tightly together as it climbed slowly but inexorably to the ceiling above, finally breaking and dispersing there.

Kay had always been struck by beauty. For a time, she had toyed with the idea of being an artist, a composer, a poet—anything that would permit her to add beauty to the world by interpreting the beauty to which she herself was exposed. Once she bought a set of oil paints and brushes and canvases and spent weeks on end trying to do on canvas what she saw with her inner eye. Another time she sat at a piano day after day trying to compose music, to elaborate upon a theme that ran through her brain. And many times she jotted down words and phrases that stubbornly refused to turn themselves into the crystal magic of poetry.

It was no use. She was no artist. She could sense, yes. She could feel and she could appreciate. But she was woefully lacking in creative talent, and she had come to recognize this fact with the passage of time. Now she was quite resigned to what she was—a person who could be extremely sensitive to beauty but who could bring no new beauty into the world.

Once this had pained her. It did so no more. She had devoted her efforts ever since to living the perfect life, a life that in itself might constitute a work of art.

Kay was pleased with the life she led.

Now, still standing by the side of the bed, she smiled thinly and reached out to pass a hand over Sue's sleeping body. She felt Sue's breasts, her belly. Kay's hands slipped lower still and touched the warm damp essence that was Sue, and the younger girl moaned and squirmed lazily in her sleep.

No.

Don't wake her.

Reluctantly Kay withdrew her hand and straightened up. The other girl slept like a lamb. Kay sighed heavily, drew again on her cigarette, and left the room.

MONA WAS STILL IN her room when the telephone rang. She had taken a shower as soon as Bart got out and left her alone, and as soon as her laughing fit had subsided and she was once again in control of herself. Then she had thought of going out to find some other damned man, but she was tired and Bart had managed to lessen her overall enthusiasm for sex, at least for the time being. She flicked the television set on and plopped herself in front of it and watched an endless parade of commercials occasionally interrupted momentarily by drama.

And then the telephone rang.

Her first reaction was that it was Bart—after all, it had been that kind of a night, hadn't it? This was a silly notion, because Bart was not exactly the type of nut who would be apt to call a girl on the phone. But this was her first reaction, and in spite of herself she started to shake and shiver.

The phone went on ringing.

It couldn't be Bart, she told herself. And if it was, well, so what? Her door was locked. If it was him, she would call the desk and they would have the house detective up there in a minute, with a truckload of Miami Beach cops on the way. She took a breath and rolled over onto her side and reached for the phone.

"Hello?"

"Hello? Mona? This is Mel."

She smiled, feeling foolish. Of course, she thought. It made sense that a straight type like Mel would call her. But a bastard like Bart would never do something like that. She smiled at the memory of Mel, his furious need for her, his hunger to please her. She remembered the way he had kissed her feet.

And an idea came to her.

"Hello," she said again. "What's on your mind, honey?"

"I'm in the lobby."

"Oh?"

"I went out for awhile, after dinner. I got bored stiff and I came back home. You know where I wound up going?"

"Where?"

"A strip show."

"Here on the Beach?"

"No, downtown in Miami. Supposed to be a real hot club because the broads peel all the way down. But who cares? All of these nuts were standing around with their eyes popping, and I was starting to fall asleep."

"That's hard to believe."

"Well, some people just like to look, Mona. But I'm not that kind. And what the hell was there to get so excited about? I've seen it all before, if you know what I mean."

"Uh-huh."

"So I came back to the hotel."

"So you did."

"I figured, well—"

Her eyes were half-lidded, dreamy. "Tell me what you thought, Mel," she said lazily.

"I figured maybe you weren't sleeping."

"I'm not."

"And I figured maybe you were alone."

"I *am* alone, Mel."

"And that, well—"

"Yes?"

He hesitated for a moment, and she grinned happily at his hesitation. He wanted to get in her pants and he didn't know how to put it nicely over the telephone.

"I'd like to come up to your room, Mona."

"You would?"

"Yes."

"Whatever for?"

"I . . . uh . . . I—"

She smiled again. Deep down inside she longed to get a sort of grim revenge in return for the indignities to which Bart had subjected her. But she couldn't take revenge out against Bart. She had to manage it by dominating some other man, and she couldn't have thought of a more perfect candidate than Mel. He almost seemed to want to be taken over and ruled by a woman, she thought. He would be ideal for what she had in mind.

"I don't know, Mel."

"You don't?"

"I mean," she went on, "it is pretty late, and—"

"It's not that late."

"Well, I've been watching a television program. I don't want to turn it off in the middle, you know."

"Mona, for goodness sake—"

"Now let me think," she said. She took a cigarette, lit it. Oh, this was perfect, she thought. He was really beginning to get a little hot under the collar, among other places. She blew out a cloud of smoke and put her red lips to the mouthpiece of the phone once more. When she spoke, she made her voice as low-pitched and husky as she possibly could.

She said, "Mel."

"What?"

"If I let you come up here—"

"Yes?"

"Well, would you be very good? Would you do everything I told you to do?"

"Uh, sure—"

"Because you can come up if you promise to be very good, Mel. But you'll have to follow all my orders. Do you understand?"

"I understand."

"Otherwise, I'll ask you to leave."

"I get it, Mona."

"Do you?"

"Sure."

"That's good," she said. "Now listen to me carefully. I don't want you to come up here right away."

"Why not?"

"I have to get ready, Mel."

"Oh, I see."

"Don't forget. You can come up in fifteen minutes.

No sooner, and not much later. Come upstairs to my room fifteen minutes from now. All right?"

"All right."

"You can have a drink in the meantime. Or you can get some coffee. But give me fifteen minutes."

"I will, Mona."

"I'll see you then, Mel," she said.

She cradled the phone and stretched her arms high over her head, delighted with herself and with Mel, delighted with everything. She dropped to the floor, turned off the television set, then reached under the bed and hauled out the trusty old tape recorder. There was a fresh reel on the spindle. She checked it over but she did not turn it on yet. He wouldn't be coming for fifteen minutes. There was no sense in wasting one-eighth of the time on the reel of tape.

She would dominate this man, she told herself. She would make him do whatever she wanted him to do and he would do it gladly, however humbling or humiliating it might be. She remembered Willie Retch, remembered how the slimy little photographer had liked to play the slave for her. But this would be different. This would be no game.

Mel would actually be her slave.

And she would rule him with an iron hand.

She walked to her dresser. She was still quite nude;

she had taken a shower when Bart left her, and she had not bothered to put on any clothing since then. On the top of the dresser she found a large bottle of especially expensive perfume. It was perfume which she used only rarely. Most of the claims which perfumes made were a lot of bull as far as she was concerned, but this particular perfume was something quite special. It was a real jungle-lust type of scent. A woman didn't dare wear it for normal use, because it made her smell as though she had just had sexual relations with three baboons, two tigers, and a whole herd of elephants. But right now, that was exactly the way she desired most to smell.

Like an oversexed Amazon.

Like a real sexual beast of a woman.

She applied the perfume much too liberally. She started off with a dab behind each ear, and then she laughed at her reticence and went wild with the crazy stuff. She doused a washcloth in it and bathed both of her breasts until they were dripping with the hot sensual scent.

More—

She rubbed a handful of the stuff onto her belly and let it drip down over her loins and the tops of her thighs. She anointed her buttocks with perfume, doused herself under the arms.

Great, she thought.

She went to the door and unlatched it so that it could

be opened from outside without a key. She went to her closet and found a pair of high-heeled shoes and put them on. She thought about wearing something else—a frilly bra, a flimsy slip, a nightie. She decided against it. The shoes were sufficient.

She walked over to the bed, removed all of the bed clothing and stretched out on her back on the bottom sheet and settled her head on her pillow. She breathed slowly and evenly and waited.

Fifteen minutes to the dot after his phone call, she heard a knock at the door. She breathed deeply and her nostrils filled with the lust-filled aroma of the perfume she wore. The whole room reeked of it. She let one hand trail down the front of her body and she rubbed herself where she was already beginning to itch so wondrously.

She said, "Come in, Mel."

Chapter Nine

WHEN SUE OPENED HER eyes she was just coming out of a slightly troublesome dream. She had been dreaming that she was in the middle of a tropical island, with short black natives around her in a circle. They were beating drums and advancing slowly toward her with daggers clutched tight in their fists. She was encircled by them, surrounded. They kept coming closer, and just as she readied herself to scream, the dream fell apart and she opened her eyes and was instantly awake.

One hellish dream, she thought. What would a psychiatrist make of something like that? She didn't know much about psychiatry or psychology so she wasn't equipped to figure it out. But it had certainly been one hell of a dream. There was no getting around the fact, no question about it.

She rolled over to look at Kay.

Kay wasn't there.

This was a surprise. In a low voice she called Kay's name, thinking that the older woman might be in the bathroom or something like that. There was no answer. With an effort Sue tossed her legs over the side of the bed and got to her feet. She checked the bathroom. It was empty. Obviously Kay had gone out. She didn't know where the woman had gone, or why, or when she might return. She was stuck in Kay's room for the time being, and she was alone, and she did not want to be alone.

Maybe it was Kay's way of telling her to go back to her own room, of saying that Kay wanted to sleep by herself that night. But that didn't make a tremendous amount of sense, did it? There would have been a simpler way for Kay to put the same message across. All Kay would have had to do was tell her that it would not be safe for her to stay the night, that her husband might begin to suspect something about the two of them.

No, that wasn't it.

Something else, then.

She lit a cigarette, sat down in an armchair and tried to think straight. How long had Kay been gone? At first she thought that there was no way to tell. Then she went over to touch Kay's side of the bed. The clothing no longer was warm with Kay's body heat. So that meant that the older woman had been gone for at least half an hour and possibly longer than that.

Why?

She began to figure it out. Suppose Kay had been unable to sleep, say. It would have been hell for Kay to stick around the room, naturally, because she would have had to remain quiet in order to let Sue go on sleeping. She couldn't have put on the television set, for instance. So, Kay would have grown restless, and she then would have simply gotten dressed and gone out for awhile.

So far so good.

But then what would happen?

There was a gay bar right across the street and a few doors down Collins, Sue remembered. And what more natural place on earth was there for a lesbian who wanted to unwind a little and couldn't stay in her room?

In all likelihood, Kay would have gone to the bar.

At which point anything might have happened.

Kay was a striking woman. Some dirty little dyke at the bar might have made a pass at her. And if Kay was in the mood, if Kay was restless and all tied up in knots, then Kay might very well have taken the little butch up on it.

Sue began to shake.

This was a new experience for her. She had never been jealous before, but now she burned with jealousy. It was blind and unreasoning jealousy. She had not realized that she cared so much for Kay, but evidently she did, and she was shaking with a mixture of fear and fury. She wanted to throw her clothes on and hurry over to the gay bar, and at the same time she was afraid to do this out of fear that she might find what she was afraid of, that she might see Kay with another girl.

But what could she do about it?

Nothing, she thought. Nothing at all, when you came right down to it. There was always the chance that Kay had not visited the gay café at all, she knew. On top of that, there was the chance that, even if she did go to the bar, nothing would come of it. So Sue had to disregard the whole possibility that Kay might meet another girl and had to decide what the hell she herself was going to do in the meantime.

She could get dressed and go downstairs for a drink, of course. But she didn't feel much like drinking, for one thing, and for another thing she didn't feel like seeing anyone. There would be a crowd at the bar, a batch of men on the make and a batch of drunken women waiting to be made, and she didn't feel as though she could stomach that sort of a mob scene. Even thinking about it made her slightly nauseous, slightly green around the gills.

What else?

Well, she could go downstairs to her own room. If Mel was still out, she could take a hot bath and get in her own bed and go to sleep.

But if he was there—

If he was there, she knew intuitively, he would want to make love to her. And his lovemaking was intolerable enough on an ordinary night. Now, after a session or three

with Kay, it would be absolutely impossible for her to allow Mel to invade the peaceful sanctuary of her fine body.

And he might insist upon it. He was like that sometimes, crazy to assert his rights as a husband, and those
were the occasions on which she gave in to him and let
him do what he had to do to her, putting up with it and
hating every moment of it. Fortunately, it didn't last long
with Mel. With Kay a bout of lust could stretch halfway
to the ends of time, but with Mel it was on-again off-again
and quickly done with and over with, and she was thank-
ful at least for that if for nothing more.

No.

Not tonight.

She couldn't possibly face that tonight, not for anything. So, since she didn't want to go out and didn't want
to go back to her room, there was only one choice open.
She had to stay where she was, in Kay's room, passing the
time somehow and trying not to think of what Kay might
be doing and waiting for Kay to come back to her and
make her happy once again.

She stretched out on the bed and closed her eyes, but
this time sleep did not come. Her hands rested on her
thighs, then moved upward along the sides of her own
body. She felt the silken satin smoothness of her flesh beneath her own hands, and it was like caressing a woman
and it was also like being caressed by a woman, both at

once, both sensations coming as one while her hands bus-
ied themselves with her own flesh.

How nice, she thought drowsily.

How very nice.

She smiled a lazy smile and yawned a ladylike yawn
and cupped her huge breasts with her dexterous hands.
She began to rub herself, busying her hands with her
breasts as if she were fondling Kay's breasts, cupping and
stroking and pinching, playing with the little nipples until
they protruded tautly from her soft-firm flesh. She teased
her nipples and the mounds of flesh upon which they
were mounted until weird bits and pieces of desire began
to run their course through her system.

How nice, she thought, for a woman to be able to
pleasure herself in this fashion. How nice it felt, her own
hands on her own body. She had done this before. Sometimes in New York she had not dared to make the rounds
of the gay bars; yet her hungers were too much to bear
and she had to find some small measure of relief. So, she
would go into the bathroom and lock the door and thrust
feverish hands beneath her skirt and find herself and toy
with herself until, shaking and trembling, she thrust and
jerked herself to an incomplete and shaky fulfillment that,
if nothing else, was at least better than no sex at all.

But this was different.

Now there was no rush, no urgency, no deep and

abiding need. And in the same fashion there was no sense of indecency about what she was doing. She was not ashamed of herself, as she had always been ashamed in the bathroom of their New York apartment. She was doing this to herself not because she had to but because she actively wanted to, and this made a tangible difference.

Her hands slid lower.

Lower.

Lower—

Her hands sought and found, reached and received, and when her hands found what they were hunting she felt little quivers of passion emanating from the secret essence of her femaleness and stretching out magnificently to every corner of her body. Faster and faster her fingers flew. Higher and higher her passion soared, until the world buckled and moaned and broke apart. Her body reached for and sought and found the last sweet measure of sexual devotion, trembling on the precipice of climax and plunging at last headlong into the yawning gaping gash of sensual fulfillment.

Mmmmmmm!

It felt so damned good she couldn't believe it.

WHEN MEL WALKED INTO the room the scent of lust hit him between the eyes like a sledgehammer. He reeled from the force of the scent that she had used. At first he thought that it was not perfume, that she had taken on a whole army of sex maniacs while he was gone. Then he saw her on the bed and he knew that it was perfume, but this did not lessen his inflammatory reactions to it. He was like a bull in the mating season, as randy and raunchy and horny, and a stallion with the stud fee already paid.

There she was.

Nude, with one hand tucked over her crotch and the other at her side.

Nude, with a pair of high-heeled shoes on her little feet.

Nude, with the scent of overpowering passion emanating from her every pore, rising up furiously from her breasts and loins.

Nude.

And waiting.

He took a step toward her, then halted. She looked at him, her face clothed neither in a smile nor in a frown.

"Wait," she said, and he stopped in his tracks.

"You have to be very good to me, Mel," she said.

"I will."

"You have to do everything I tell you."

"I will, Mona." The words came out in a croak and he barely recognized his own voice. It was as though someone else was forcing words through his lips.

"Do you like me, Mel?"

"Yes!"

"Do you like the way I look?"

"Yes."

"Do you think I'm beautiful?"

"Yes."

"Good. Take off all your clothes, Mel. Take off everything. And I want you to be neat about it, Mel. Take off all of your clothes and hang them neatly over the chair. Go ahead, Mel. Remember, you have to do everything I say."

There was something awfully exciting about all of this, he thought. Something terribly breathtaking about the idea of being utterly dominated by this little tramp. He was her slave, and he did not mind the role. God, how lovely she was! He would do anything she asked, anything, if only she would grant him temporary possession of her succulent flesh.

He undressed. He hung his sport jacket over the back of the chair, took off his tie, unbuttoned his shirt and pulled it loose from the waistband of his slacks. He removed his shirt and put it on the chair, then untied each shoe in turn and took them off and set them on the floor in front of the chair. He took off his socks and tucked them into his shoes. He loosened his belt and unzipped his pants and took them off, folding them neatly over an arm of the chair. He peeled off his undershorts and put them, too, on the chair, and stood naked in front of her.

"You're excited, aren't you, Mel?"

He nodded, mute.

"I can tell when you're excited, Mel. You get very big and hard when you're excited. Am I making you get like that?"

He nodded again. He knew that he could not speak. He tried to force himself to say something, anything, but his mouth opened and the words refused to come out. He felt like an awful fool. He shut his mouth and waited.

"Mel."

He looked at her.

"Get on your knees, Mel. Crawl to me."

It was humiliating, but he did not dare offer any protest. Without a word he dropped to his hands and knees and began to crawl quickly to the foot of the bed.

"Not so fast, Mel!"

He crawled more slowly. It was an agony for him but he forced himself to crawl as slowly as he could. At last, he reached the foot of the bed.

"Kiss my shoes, Mel."

He planted burning kisses all over her shoes. How shapely they were, he marveled. How smooth the leather was. He thought how fine it would be to stretch out on the floor and let her walk all over him, stabbing into his flesh with her high-heeled shoes. The fantasy made him dizzy.

"More, Mel."

Her words were a command. He gripped her by her ankles and ran his tongue all over each shoe in turn. He took the spikes of the heels between his lips and his head spun with hunger.

"Now take my shoes off, Mel."

He took her shoes off.

"Now kiss my feet, Mel. Wait a moment. You want to kiss them, don't you, Mel?"

"Yes!"

"Tell me about it, Mel."

"I . . . I want to kiss your feet."

"Tell me all about it."

"I want to kiss your beautiful feet." He was babbling like an idiot now. "I want to kiss them, I want to kiss your toes, I want to lick them, I want to be your slave, I want to belong to you, I want to do everything to you. I want to kiss your feet; I want to kiss your feet—"

"Go ahead, Mel."

Chapter Ten

MONA WAS DRUNK WITH power. She lay on the bed while Mel kissed her feet and her head swam deliriously with feelings of unaccustomed power and domination.

This was something new.

And she enjoyed it.

In a way, this was the feeling she had when she began to blackmail a man who had been her lover. The feeling of being utterly in control, the feeling of having a male entirely dependent upon her. They came crawling to her with their blackmail money just as Mel had come crawling to kiss her feet. It was the same thing in essence, but the sexual aspects of the present fun and games rendered the entire affair far more exciting.

He was her slave, anxious to do her bidding.

She was his mistress, ready to grant him her favors only if he satisfied her every whim.

And the world was boiling over with perversion and depravity, and she was queen of the whole world, a hot bodied queen with her crown between her ripe thighs, a nymphomaniacal queen who would rule over every nook and cranny of the universe before she dragged it all down into the pit with her.

She felt the tender touch of his long tongue between her toes. It might have tickled, but she was too caught up in lust and passion and sin for any sensation to tickle. She flexed the muscles in her tiny feet and he went on doing what she was forcing him to do, and she felt hungers rise up within her, a tidal wave of passion that would in time drag them both down to drown them in a sea of perverted love.

This was what she needed. Bart had made a sexual toy out of her, and she could only hope to regain her self-respect by reversing the process, by stepping out of the role of slave and into the role of Queen of Lust.

And she was doing just that.

"Stop," she said finally.

At first he could not stop. He went on slobbering over her little feet, kissing everywhere.

"Stop!"

He stopped.

"Now stand up!"

He got to his feet, a dumb and servile expression on his face. She let her eyes run over his smoothly sculptured body. He was athletic with a broad chest, a stomach fairly trim, with legs well-muscled. At the juncture where his thickly corded thighs joined together could be seen his proud lance of Apollo. Even as Mel Dalton walked, the outthrust lance could be seen wavering in eager desire. That was good. Mona liked it when a man was so hot, he could hardly control himself. It made him a slave to a woman who was the only means of relief.

Mona looked him over carefully. The humiliation of kissing her feet had not dampened his ardor in the least. If anything, Mel was even more under her sexual spell than before.

Mona was flushed with pride.

She was filled with dynamic power.

In a few moments, her Amazon power would dominate this masculine looking athlete and humble him until he acknowledged her as the supreme Master. She would squeeze him in the tight grip and compel him to degrade himself even further—as a means of providing pleasure for her own perverted self. Only when Mona dominated a man could such a sweet joy be possible.

"Stand up."

Mel Dalton had knelt before her in a strange worshipful motion. "Yes . . ." he said thickly.

"Walk across the room." Mona folded both soft arms across her twin balloons.

Mel did as ordered, walking all around the room,

feeling the way Mona looked at every part of his naked masculinity.

"Now stand before me," she ordered.

His face moist with sexual tension, his strong body trembling, his thickly corded muscles bulging with yearning. He was breathing heavily. His throat was parched dry. Hammering at the base of his temples accentuated his inner desires. Mel's heart slammed high up in his throat.

Mona moved slowly, letting her heavy breasts dance like pagan savages in the moonlight. Then she used her hands to explore him, deliberately tweaking and pinching. She knew he was in the throes of agony and that each touch on his manhood was like fire on the flesh.

When she was done, she stood back. "Spread your legs apart, slave."

MEL DALTON REACTED WITH immediate obedience. His strong thighs parted. His buttocks were bunched muscles of strength—but his manhood was now throbbing with yearning and appeared to be a tower of power. "Y-yes, Master," in a voice that was not his own.

"You realize that I am master and you are my slave?"

"Y-yes." He was breathing heavily. His moist and perspired face was flushed with a new sense of embarrassment he never before experienced. While Mel Dalton had never been boyishly ashamed of nudity, he now felt a strange exhilaration of sensual shame by being so exposed before the pink-and-white beauty who was dominating him.

Mona reached behind to pick up an object from the small bureau. She held it tightly and then brought it out before her.

Mel's eyes opened wide with fear. He licked his dry lips. His heart pounded furiously. He dared not speak. He watched Mona come close.

"Do you see this?"

HE NODDED NUMBLY. What would she do to him? He wanted to flee in panic. But his naked feet were rooted to the floor.

"It's a letter opener—more like a sharp dagger." Her soft finger teased the sharply pointed edge of the gleaming letter opener. "I can use it the way I use a knife," she said with deliberate slowness. "With just one slash, I can slice away your manhood."

"N-no!" He reacted with terror. He yearned to close his thighs by an instinctive gesture to protect his most precious possession. "N-no—I beg you—no!" His voice became shrill.

Mona smiled. Suddenly, she lashed forward—the knife swooped up and then came down in a slash.

Mel Dalton gave a horrible shriek! Both of his hands

instinctively clutched his groin—then he looked down as if to convince himself that he was still a man.

Mona's derisive laughing echoed in his ears. "Thought I did it, eh? Well, that's just a scare—the next time, I'll really fix your manhood."

Mel Dalton's strong thighs were joined together now, locked as a wall to protect himself. But he was so shaken by the experience, he was standing there before Mona, shivering nakedly, his proud athletic body looking strangely humbled and humiliated, even though it was still splendidly masculine and virile.

But this raw terror of the experience had not bent his fierce lust for her, Mona saw. Soon, she thought, it would be time to bestow a reward upon him. She wanted him. He wanted her. It was nearly time to cap the performance with a fierce round of lust. But it was going to be different.

It was going to be sheer pleasure for Mona.

As for Mel Dalton, he was the instrument for her pleasure and nothing more. If he experienced anything from what he would be compelled to do to her, it mattered little.

But not yet.

"Tell me, slave," she spoke in a throaty whisper, "what do men do if they're without women?"

"W-what?" His voice cracked. He had to swallow hard.

"You heard me—suppose you're without a woman. How do you find relief?"

Now Mel experienced even greater embarrassment. It had always been a shameful remembrance of his early youth when he had no recourse but to relieve himself. It was so embarrassing, he felt humiliated that a beautiful goddess such as Mona would be asking about it.

"I'm waiting . . ."

"W-well, we usually—you know—all boys do it . . . sometimes in front of the other boys, or alone."

"Describe it to me. And show me how you do it with your hands . . . but don't actually do it—I don't want the firecracker to explode just yet."

Mel Dalton then went through the motions. At times, when Mona so ordered, he made vocal descriptions of just how this guilt-ridden practice was done and how he felt—from the start until the very finish. Mel was even ordered to tell of a few actual experiences, where it was done, under what circumstances.

By the time Mel finished telling all the details, he was so shaken up, so completely degraded and embarrassed, he wanted to hide somewhere. But there was no escape. Neither did he want to escape—he was so turgid with flaming desire that if he did not obtain relief, he would surely be compelled to duplicate his childhood actions.

"Kneel down," commanded Mona. She saw his burning desires and knew it would be foolish to delay any longer. As for herself, she was now trembling with an awesome power she never before experienced. Dominating males had introduced her to a new sphere of ecstasy. It was an aphrodisiac!

Clumsily, Mel Dalton got to his knees. His proud lance of power was sensuous in heat. His broad shoulders rippled with muscular contortions. He was a proud male. He was fully masculine with a rock-hard body—but he had been dominated by a conquering goddess with naked creamy flesh that drove him wild with desire.

MONA'S SMOOTH LEGS AND thighs moved toward him. She was dazzling as she came very close to her kneeling slave. "You desire me?" she asked tauntingly.

"Y-yes." He nodded, unable to speak further. Kneeling before Mona, he was so filled with urgency, he could no longer control himself.

Mona opened her thighs wide, snapped them shut, opened them and closed them, then opened them again.

Mel's eyes looked as if they were going to pop clear out of his head. His brow was wet. His hands trembled.

Now Mona came very, very close. Her hands balanced her body as she placed both palms on Mel's shoulders. Kneeling, he made a good object of balance. Looking up, he stared wildly at the spectacle of both of her massive breasts dangling from her expansive rib cage. The red strawberries were erect, moist and softly smooth. Her sylph-like body, bent at the waist, was a picture of Grecian passion.

"Love me, slave—love me—"

Mel was numbed into a shock. Now he knew what she wanted. But he had never done anything like this before. He heard it was queer.

Queers did it to each other. Boy queers and girl queers. She was asking him to . . .

"Hurry—hurry!" When she saw the slight hesitation, her trembling voice became urgent. "If you don't . . . I'll fix it so you'll never be any good to anyone—that knife—it'll slice away what you need . . ."

Mel's body trembled. He could not speak. Suddenly, he felt his head being pushed forward by Mona's hands. He tangled in the forbidden forest. Then the taboo grotto yawned wide.

He plunged within.

It rocked both of their bodies.

The licking fires erupted into a volcano.

Both of their bodies felt the spewed forth lava—the hot molten sea had splashed through their bodies. But it was not enough for Mona. She sobbed hysterically, urging him on and on and on . . .

Only once did she voice a command—and it was directed to Mel Dalton—the slave—who was ordered to perform his own relief—and Mona watched in a crazed sea of passion.

The floodgates opened and poured forth—and both were drenched in its hot lava.

MEL DALTON COULDN'T understand it.

He had always been a normal man. He liked women. A lot of them liked him. When he was alone with a woman they did what all normal people did. They made love, and it worked out well, and that was all there was to it. He had never thought of himself as a pervert. He had never had any particular desire to do things that he regarded as perversions. He couldn't even understand how that sort of thing could be exciting to a man. It just didn't make any sense to him at all. He had never been able to think it out, and so he had never spent much time worrying about it. He lived his own life, and it was a good life, a normal life, and that was the only thing that mattered.

Until now.

Until he had met Mona.

And even with Mona, everything had been perfectly normal the first time around. Just a guy and a gal, both of them hot to go at it, both of them hungry for each other, both of them getting plenty of pleasure and giving as good as they got. All in all, Mona was the most exciting broad he had ever had, but everything about that excitement had been completely normal.

But now he wasn't himself any more, and he was certainly not normal. Now he was as crazy as all the perverts in the world. All the nuts whom he had never before been able to figure out. He had crawled to her on his hands and knees. He had slobbered over her little feet and over her high-heeled shoes like a complete and total nut. And he had done to her what she ordered. He never thought he could have gone all the way like that.

Maybe he was turning queer! Everything was so confused he did not know what to think.

What was the matter with him?

What was she doing to him?

He was going crazy. He was losing his mind over the little bitch. It was as she had said—she was mistress and he was slave, utterly dominated by the beautiful red-haired witch, utterly in her power and at her mercy.

And, what was worst of all, he loved it!

That was the part that was so impossible to understand. She had a stranglehold on him. She could wreck him and ruin him at her slightest whim. And he got a real kick out of this, got true pleasure from her domination.

It wasn't normal.

Not at all.

It was a far cry from normal.

It was perverted and twisted and sick and rotten and degrading and humiliating and revolting. It was simply disgusting, truly stomach-churning and gut-turning, and that didn't make it the slightest bit easier for him to get out from under the fury of her power. No, he was caught, caught completely and utterly, and he would be her slave forever until she released him.

Now, for the moment at least, their roles were reversed from a purely physical standpoint. Now she lay on her back with her knees in the air and he was between those knees, cushioned by her breasts and her thighs, locked in place by her arms and legs, his furious manhood surging again and again into the yawning gap of her powerful lust.

The odor of her perfume raped his nostrils and clogged his lungs. The scene of her lust-gushing body was everywhere. Her breasts throbbed beneath his chest, pounding out a rhythm older than the seven seas. Her legs squeezed tight against his hips as if they were trying to cut him in two.

And he thrust at her with all the strength in his being, faster and faster and faster, harder and harder and harder, probing deeper and ever deeper into the sugar sweet essence of her naked burning passion.

More.

And more.

And even more.

Outside the wind lashed at the palm trees and stirred up high waves on the pounding surf. Inside the creak of the bedsprings was louder than the roar of the wind, and the lust of their embrace brought with it the air of the jungle in the mating season. Faster and faster their bodies moved, and he felt her hips heaving and bucking beneath him, and somehow the whole huge impossible world stole away and got lost.

It was everything and it was nothing. It was the best of times and it was the worst of times, the highest of moments and the most depraved of moments. It was heaven and it was hell, it was alpha and it was omega, it was good and it was bad, high and low, in and out, back and forth, yin and yang, up and down.

Faster.

And faster.

And faster still.

Their mouths locked in a kiss, and his tongue stole into her mouth, and her teeth closed on his tongue and bit at it hard enough to draw blood, and instead of drawing back in horror he seized on the pain and relished it, enjoying it and letting the pain spur his passion even more. Her nails raked his back, stabbing him like a shower of needles, and this pain too only served to make him thunder more and more crazily into her. She nipped at his ear lobe, crushed him between her thighs, and he pounded away at her just as the surf outside pounded incessantly at the sandy shore.

Harsher.

And deeper.

And more, more—more—

Until the crest was reached.

Then it was everything at once. It was Vesuvius erupting, it was Chicago burning, it was San Francisco quaking. It was Hiroshima and Nagasaki after the A bombs fell. It was the world caving in and crashing down and turning in upon itself with the echo of a thousand centuries of hellish fury piling one upon the other in a crescendo of unholy lust that reverberated in his brain with a furious vengeance until the whole world went black and he collapsed, spent, exhausted, upon her evil flesh.

Chapter Eleven

Kay had not gone to the gay bar across the street after she slipped out of bed and left Sue sleeping in her room. She had considered this briefly, but she changed her mind quickly. She had already made marvelous lesbian love with Sue, and that was enough for one day.

So she didn't go looking for a woman.

Instead, she went looking for a man.

The older woman stood smoking a cigarette in the lobby, smiling quietly to herself. Actually, she thought, she had not been entirely honest with Sue. She had led Sue to think that she was exclusively homosexual, and this was by no means the truth. Kay had always been a profound searcher after sensual pleasures, and she had learned at an early age that she was not the type of person who could confine her experiments to a single sex any more than she could limit her sexual affections to a single person. She had slept with men, and she greatly enjoyed it. She had also slept with women, and she enjoyed that as well.

She could understand a woman like Sue, a lesbian to the core, a woman who could only love other women and who could not abide a man touching her or piercing her with his sword of flesh. She could understand such women, and she could desire them.

She could also understand women who were exclusively heterosexual, women who would shrink at the thought of sex with another female, women who were strongly and solely attracted to men. She could understand these women as well, and she shared their desires very definitely.

But she could not completely go along with either type of woman. Sex was a magnificent affair, the most important aspect of life for an individual who wanted to live a complete and creative existence. And as far as she was concerned, it was sheer nonsense to limit your enjoyment of sex either to women or to men. A thoroughgoing bisexual, Kay had found herself capable of strong attachments to men as well as to women, responses that provided maximum pleasure regardless of the sex of her partner of the moment. As far as she could see, a person who swung from both sides of the plate got twice as many hits and drove in three times as many runs. She was a switch-hitter, and she felt that it was the only way for her to live.

Why limit yourself? Why stick to men and miss your chance at the soft sweet bodies and warm willing mouths of women? Why stick to women and miss the hard thrusts and deep pleasures which men were so capable of providing?

No, it was silly to give up either variety of pleasure, and she did not intend to do so. She had the son in the morning and the daughter at night, and she liked it that way. She had taken sweet pleasure from the smooth sweet body of Sue Dalton and now, since she was too restless to sleep, she would seek a different sort of pleasure with a man.

But first she had to find a man.

It would be amusing, she thought, if she could find Sue Dalton's husband Mel. There would be true poetry in something like that, seducing the wife in the afternoon and having the husband, as it were, for dessert. Sooner or later, she planned to make a try for Mel Dalton. Sue had described her husband quite vividly, trying to make him sound like an absolute ogre, and yet all the qualities which seemed so dreadful to Sue made the man sound all the more exciting to Kay. Kay liked her women submissive, but she liked rough strong men who acted like men, and Mel sounded as though he would be ideal.

Now, though, it might be hard to find him. Now she would have to settle for any man who came along, at least any man who promised to be more than a little exciting. She was no nymphomaniac. She wouldn't go with a man just because he was a man and available. Oh, if she hadn't had any sex in awhile, then she might lower her standards somewhat. But she didn't have to lower them now. Her basic physical needs had been quite satisfied by Sue, and she could afford to wait until she met a man who appealed to her strongly enough for her to go with him.

FIRST SHE TRIED THE Banzai Hotel's bar. That had been fine cruising ground that afternoon, when she met Sue, but tonight it was too crowded, too noisy, and too depressing as far as she was concerned. She had one drink, paid for it, fended off a pair of men with big ideas and little else to recommend them, and left the hotel for the beach outside.

The night was beautiful. Waves crashed violently against the sandy shore. The wind was strong, not of hurricane proportions, certainly, but blowing hard enough to add excitement to the darkness of the night. She kicked off her shoes and walked barefoot along the beach, loving the feel of the sand between her toes, abandoning herself entirely to the delicious enjoyment of the night and the surf and the wind and the sand.

It was an odd place to be looking for a man, but Kay was not so desperately driven by sexual need as to be willing to give up the pleasures of her walk to chase after male companionship. She decided to walk until she was tired, then to go try some other hotel bar to look for a lover.

But she didn't have to.

Because she found a lover on the beach.

She heard him before she saw him. She heard someone swimming in the angry surf, and her first thought was that he had to be out of his mind. The ocean was dangerous at night, especially on a moonless and starless night like this one. The waves were high, and there was undoubtedly a vicious undertow. Besides, everyone knew that barracuda swam dangerously close to shore when the beaches were dark. A man could lose an arm to one bite of a barracuda, and a school of them could turn a man into a skeleton in minutes.

So that was her first thought—that the man was a lunatic who was taking ridiculous chances with his life. But she stopped in her tracks and listened to him swimming, and another thought entered her mind.

Sure, maybe the man was crazy. But he was also very brave, and he was probably strong as a bull, and it was a damned good bet that he would know what to do with a woman.

Ahhhh.

She had been carrying her shoes. She dropped them to the sand and sank to the sand beside them. She hovered in the darkness, waiting for the man to emerge from the water. Her heart began beating hard within the confines of her rib cage. Her breasts rose and fell with her rapid and intense breathing. She was excited now, excited at the idea of this man, excited at the notion of coupling furiously on the dark beach, furiously and wordlessly, with loins giving up pleasure to loins and the surf pounding a few feet away from them and the wind lashing at their bare bodies.

She waited.

Breathlessly.

Desperately.

Until at last he swam in toward shore, and she saw him rise in the water, strong and large, with a bull's neck and broad shoulders thickly corded with muscle. She watched in total silence as he clambered slowly forth out of the water and onto the beach. She was not surprised to note that he had gone in without a bathing suit. Men who swim at night in the ocean do not bother with swim trunks.

Of course, that meant taking an awful chance. Suppose a barracuda swam in close. One snap of those powerful jaws could change a man's life rather drastically.

But she was gratified to note that this had not happened to the man who was now emerging from the water. He was as much a man as ever, and his dimensions in this respect were enviable. A huge stallion of a man. He looked as though he could tear a woman in two, ripping her up the middle and splitting her at the seams.

Kay shivered with delight.

He didn't notice her at first. He came up on the sandy beach and she waited until he was a scant ten feet away from her. Then she said, "Hello, there."

Most men would have jumped.

This one didn't. Instead, he turned around slowly, completely matter-of-fact about his nakedness. He looked at her and his lips tightened into an odd grin. She looked at his eyes. They were deeply sunken into his skull, and the effect was that of a death's head gleaming at her in the darkness.

She got to her feet. While he stood there, hands on hips, his eyes upon her, she removed her clothing. She did this without a word, peeling herself completely naked. Now they would do it, she thought.

Now he would have her.

Here.

On the sand, with the wind lashing at them and the surf a few yards away.

Now—

He stayed where he was and she approached him slowly, slowly but surely, her feet sinking into the sand with each step. Her heart was pounding wildly. There was something truly awesome about the way he stood there, his face a mask, his eyes sunk deep in his head, his hands on his hips, just waiting—

She moved very close to him. She saw the sharp delineation of his muscles. She smelled the masculine smell of him, salty from the ocean water.

She said, "My name is Kay."

"I'm Bart," he said.

"Is that for Barton or Bartholomew?"

"Just Bart is plenty," he said.

And then his fist lashed out hard and he caught her full force in the pit of the stomach.

MEL LAY WITH HIS eyes closed and his flesh utterly exhausted. He heard Mona moving near him but he could not open his eyes. He felt as he had never felt before, drained completely and utterly, empty, broken, wasted. He felt depraved, and this was a new feeling for him, and one of which he was not at all proud. He had done things which he had never done before that night, and he had felt as he had never felt before that night, and the whole thing was too much for him to even begin to comprehend. He was lost, and he didn't know what to do or which way to turn, and he wanted to crawl in a hole and pull the hole in after him.

"Mel."

His eyes opened.

"Now you're my slave forever," she said.

"Yes."

"Did you like what we did?"

"I—"

"Tell me, Mel."

"I don't know."

"You certainly acted as though you liked it."

"I did and I didn't. I . . . enjoyed making love to you—"

"That was fairly obvious."

"But I hated myself. I . . . I never did anything like this before. No woman had power over me the way you do."

"That's because you're my slave."

"I suppose so."

"I know so. Get up, Mel."

It took almost superhuman effort for him to drag himself out of bed. He wanted to stay where he was. He wanted to sleep until the weariness left his mind and body, until he felt alive again, until he could think straight once more. But her slightest wish was his command. The fact that he had assuaged his sexual hungers had nothing to do with it. He still had to obey her. Whatever she demanded of him he had to give.

He got up. He started to sag once, but he caught hold of himself and managed somehow to stay on his feet. He looked at her, at her naked body, and for a moment he surprised himself when a short rush of desire inflamed him. But this passed, and he stood looking at her like a helpless slave.

A humiliated, dominated slave.

"You should go back to your room now, Mel."

"I don't want to."

"Maybe your wife wants you, Mel."

"I don't care."

"Don't you care about your wife, Mel?"

"No."

"Don't you love her?"

"I hate her."

She smiled like a cat. "Who do you care about, Mel?"

"You."

"Only me?"

"Only you."

"Suppose I had another man, and I made him make love to me and made you watch. What would you do?"

"I don't know."

The thought of another man on top of her flesh made his hackles rise.

"You would watch, Mel."

"I would watch," he said dully.

"You would do whatever I told you to do, Mel."

"I would do whatever you told me to do."

She yawned and stretched. "Get me a cigarette, Mel." He got her a cigarette. "Now light it for me, Mel."

HE LIT THE CIGARETTE and gave it to her. She took it from him and smoked. He wanted a cigarette, but he was afraid to take one, as if she might not allow him to smoke in her royal presence. But she told him to go ahead and have a cigarette for himself, and he took one from her pack and lit it.

"Look at you," she said. "Your back is scratched to ribbons. All cuts and scratches and dried blood. Who could have done something like that to you, Mel?"

"You did it."

Her laughter was loud in his ears, like the shrill cry of a vulture. "Yes," she cried, "I did it, didn't I, Mel? And tell me something else, Mel. Did you like it?"

"Yes," he said. And he hated himself.

Chapter Twelve

When Bart hit her, Kay doubled up in agony and clutched her hands to her naked belly. Her legs went weak and she began to fall forward. She didn't know what was happening, or why. She fell toward him and he caught her by her shoulders and held her with one hand and slapped her three times across the face with his other hand. He hit her so hard that her teeth rattled.

He shoved her, then, and she went reeling along the beach until she collapsed onto the sand. She shook her head to clear it, raised her head to see him coming purposefully after her, covering the distance between them swiftly with long sure strides. She started to get up. He caught up with her and spun her around to face him. He drew a hand back and slapped her across the breasts. She howled with pain.

He laughed. His laughter drowned out her scream. He slapped her again, and she looked down and saw an ugly red mark that his hand had left on her breast. She was terrified. The man was an utter maniac, a crazy person. If she wasn't lucky he would kill her, and there was nothing she could do about it.

But why?

She had done nothing to him. She had come to him readily, greedy for his embrace, anxious to be possessed by him. And he was repaying her with brutality and wickedness, and she could not understand it at all.

It made no sense.

It was mad.

And so was he.

Then, suddenly, he began to speak to her. "You're like all women," he was saying. "Cheap and rotten and evil. You stink inside and out. You smell like rotten fish. You're cheap and low and lousy and you deserve whatever happens to you."

Then he brought up his knee into the pit of her stomach again. A low sob escaped her lips. She doubled up in pain and his hand lashed out and caught her on the point of the jaw. She saw stars even though the night was starless, and she fell back and went sprawling on her butt in the sand.

Well, that settled all doubts. The lunatic hated women. God knew why. Maybe his mother had been a tramp. Maybe he had walked in on her at an impressionable age when she was going down on some man or something. Maybe he tried to make it with a woman once and couldn't rise to the occasion. Maybe he was just born rotten, with a disease in his brain.

Oh, there were any number of possibilities. But it didn't do her very much good to contemplate them. It did no good at all, if the truth be known. Because when you came right down to it, he was a crazy man and she was at his mercy. He could do whatever he wanted to her. She had no choice but to endure whatever it was that he planned to do.

He came to her, hauled her to her feet again. He slapped her breasts and kneed her at the very bottom of her belly and made her moan sickly.

Go ahead, she thought.

Get it over with.

"There's only one thing to do with women like you," he told her.

What would it be?

"Just one thing," he went on.

And then he shoved her once more and sent her sprawling, and she started to get up, got as far as getting up onto her hands and knees, and then all at once he was behind her, his hands on her body, and she felt his thighs against her buttocks and his hands on her bare flesh.

"Like this," he said.

All at once she knew. And she thought of what he was going to do to her, and she remembered the size of him, the awful size of him, and she went fish belly white with terror. She felt his massive maleness against her and she recoiled in shock.

His hands moved to grip her big breasts. He squeezed them, and she felt the astonishing pressure of his strong fingers on her softness, and a low moan escaped her lips. Then his hands left her breasts and left them aching with the memory of his touch. His hands moved now to her buttocks.

She gasped. He squeezed her buttocks, squeezed them hard in his big hands. He pulled them apart and probed at her, then pressed them hard together, then yanked them once more apart.

And pushed.

And pressed.

At first she thought it would be impossible. He could never do it, it was impossible. It would be easier to jam a camel through the eye of a needle than to do what he had it in mind to do. But he was determined and she was defenseless. He went on stabbing blindly but persistently at her. The gap widened. She moaned and cried and died inside. He came on stronger and stronger. She felt pain shrieking like a sword slicing through silk, and then, horribly, he had her.

When he first entered her she was certain that she was going to die. He was very large. His target was very small. The pain was so huge, so overpowering, that she thought for sure it would kill her and they would find her bloody body on the beach in the morning, dead, lifeless—

It didn't kill her.

It hurt. How it hurt! And when he began to move with her and within her the pain increased and she knew she could not bear any more pain, that it would be simply too much for her.

If it got any worse, she thought, then there was no question about it: she would surely die. It got worse.

She didn't die.

And then, miraculously, something happened. Then, all at once, it stopped getting worse and it began to get better. It was, in a way, like the time she had lost her virginity to a man. The pain had been terrible at first, although nowhere near this in intensity, and then little by glorious little the pain had subsided and pleasure had taken its place. Strangely enough, this was precisely what was happening now. The original trauma of penetration had faded into the background. The movements he was making, more violent than ever, had ceased to be painful and had begun to grow progressively more pleasurable.

It got better.

And better.

And better.

Her whole body began to tremble. Not from fear, not now. Not from pain. No, her excitement was true physical excitement, and she felt a flurry of joy at this sensation, one she had heard of but one she had never before experienced. She moved in time with his motions. He redoubled his energy and attacked her rounded rump with furious abandon. All of this only served to pitch her passion higher and ever higher, up and up and away, sending her soaring hysterically through time and space to the furthest reaches of the Universe.

When the end came, the finale, the coda, the sexual Valhalla, her body shook and trembled like a leaf in a hurricane, racked with spasms in a special portion of her body that had never before been the source of pleasure. She groaned and moaned and laughed and cried and came hard and fast and good. He withdrew from her and she sprawled on her face in the sand and wept sweet tears of unfamiliar fulfillment.

He left her without a word. She heard his footsteps for a moment in the sand, and then he was gone. She stayed where she was, resting, letting things come back to some reasonable facsimile of normalcy. She breathed deeply, calmed herself, and rejoiced in this new path to sexual joy.

Then she plunged into the cool ocean, washing the sand from her skin, washing his lust from her flesh. When she returned to the beach and dried herself and dressed, she still ached from his brutal assault. Her breasts were sore, and the pit of her stomach was sore. She was terribly sore where he had loved her.

But in spite of all this she felt absolutely and utterly and thoroughly divine.

BART WAS PARTIALLY EXHAUSTED. He strode nakedly across the sandy beach, feeling the pride of a satisfied stallion who had mounted a female and proved himself the superior sex. But there were still some slight tremblings which Bart associated with a yearning to repeat the same act—if he could find another unwilling victim.

Yes, she had to be unwilling.

He wanted a girl who would put up a fight while he tore off her clothes and then brutally tweaked, pinched and pulled at her responsive flesh. It would inflame his desires more than anything else.

Bart felt the velvet night blackness cloak him. The surf was mild now. From the distance, even in the swirling shadows of night, there could be seen a white sail or two. Sex in the middle of the ocean. It sounded exciting. A world of your own. A world in which you could do what you wanted to your helpless victims.

Bart strolled aimlessly. He closed his eyes. He breathed deeply. The salt-bitten night air was tangy and refreshing. Still keeping his eyes closed, he kept on walking and walking, not caring where he would go. He even forgot that he was stark naked and might happen upon a group of night bathers who were clothed.

Bart was proud of his manhood. He always nursed a secret desire to expose himself. He had thrilled at beach clubs, locker rooms, private dressing places; it meant he had a legitimate reason for baring himself and letting others look at his nakedness.

It gave him a feeling of confidence about his superior endowments. If they made ribald comments and feinted grabbing catches at his manhood, so much better. In fact, he thrilled if someone had made a snatch and caught up his powers. *They* usually reacted with embarrassment since men are not supposed to be so interested in one another. But it made Bart all the more proud.

"Hey—lookit this!"

With a shock, Bart was roused out of his reverie. He opened his eyes. Where was he?

"Wow—a real hunk of man. Look at all that . . ."

"Hey—get out of my way!" Bart found himself surrounded by three young men. They looked like the beachcomber types, the ones who sold their bodies to Miami tourists—male or female or both—and made a living out of it. Bart felt a flush of embarrassment to be accosted by them.

Something warned him.

"Who's in your way?" The spokesman for the trio was

a bare-chested blond Adonis type—the he-man that lonely women (and men, too) would snap up at any asking price. He was naked except for a pair of tight-fitting chino shorts. These had once been trousers but were raggedly cut just below his crotch. There was no disputing the fact that the blond kid was a real man.

"Are we in your way?"

Bart saw that he had stumbled into a small beach party, so to speak. A small fire had been built and the trio were roasting franks and potatoes. A rickety cot had been erected. Maybe they would spend the night here. They were little better than hoboes, despite their youth.

"I said, get out of my way." Bart bunched both fists together and the muscles in his biceps bulged out.

"Hey—that's *all* man, too!" Another young beach comber, thick black hair, combed in a pseudo-Beatle cut around his good-looking face, reached out and stroked Bart's upper arm. This one wore a pair of skin-tight blue jeans that had seen their better days. He was obviously naked underneath.

"I want it first!" The last of the trio was more like a heavy built truckdriver. His massive body was elephantine but solid muscle. His face was ill-matched. It was angelic. Almost feminine in softness. Even his voice had a swishy quality. "I like men."

"Then have a ball among yourselves!" Bart was getting angered, annoyed and admittedly frightened. He did not like the way they had encircled him and the intimate way their rough hands were fondling his back, naked buttocks and even between his legs. "Want me to holler for the cops?" It was a stupid thing for Bart to say. This placed him on the defensive.

The blond youth laughed. His silky blond hair was bleached white by the Miami sun. "Holler until your lungs run dry, buddy. This here's the Cove—deserted at this hour of the night. Didn't you bring a road map with you? Fine time to decide to go sunbathing—in your birthday suit at midnight!"

The Cove? Bart thought he remembered hearing about this out-of-the-way nook along the shore. Daytimes, it was used by fisherman who wanted to get away from it all. Nightly, it was isolated—except for lovers who wanted an orgy under the moon and be certain of privacy. It was scarcely, if ever, patrolled.

Bart cursed himself. He should have kept his eyes open.

"You guys looking for trouble?" he snapped. Both of his thighs were instinctively drawn together as if fearing the worst. He felt vulnerable in his nakedness.

"Unh, unh," mumbled the dark-haired boy with a strange smile on his youthful face. Even by firelight, the strength of his body was all too plain. "We're looking for something else—fun."

The blond boy spoke up. "Suppose you just set yourself down, Nature Boy, and let's get acquainted."

The movements of the trio were so sudden, Bart hardly had a second to calculate protective steps. One moment he felt himself being kicked off his feet. Someone's foot lashed out. Bart went hurtling backwards. Arms seized him, dragged him over to the cot. They worked swiftly. Bart punched and kicked but he was outnumbered. Hands secured him to the cot—spreadeagled him—with thick mooring ropes chafing his wrists and elbows.

Bart was bound—nakedly—face down!

"Real big muscle man, too." From above, hands explored his back, then his buttocks. "Let's get him all worked up."

The trio laughed with joy. They had a plaything now and were going to have a good time. Hands were everywhere. Moist invasions were so intimate that Bart twitched. His body erupted into spasms.

"Cut that out!" Now he was growing hysterical. His head hung over the cot's edge. He stared down at the dark sand. If he twisted his head, he saw their dark shapes dancing around him. But the more he pulled at his bonds, the tighter they grew. "Let me loose!"

"Not yet," laughed one of the boys who then inserted his hands right beneath the most intimate portion of Bart's body and fingered him so delicately that he could not help but become aroused. "Say—you're getting worked up." The trio made ribald remarks. The boy who fondled Bart then reported, to the most intimate detail, about Bart's manhood.

A scream escaped Bart's throat. "Hey—you're killing me." His bravado had melted now that he met his equals.

"Yeah," a voice from above warned, "don't spoil it—not yet anyway."

"Let's see how strong he is," the blond youth said, brushing back his sun-bleached hair from his handsome face. "Some of those New York tourists like me to do it this way—makes 'em all worked up."

There were whispers, giggles and a strange sensuous air about everything. Then Bart, in his spread-eagled, face down bondage, heard a belt buckle. There was an awesome silence. Suddenly, a whistling sound pierced the night air.

A shock ripped across Bart's broad shoulders. He screamed.

"More, more!" someone urged.

The thick leather belt swung through the air. It slashed across the muscular shoulders again. The flesh responded with thick contortions. Bart screamed. Fire tore across his back.

He was being flogged!

"Lookit the way the muscles bulge up—make those hips bounce! C'mon, make 'em bounce and dance—get 'em all worked up!"

The trio were crazed with sadistic lust. The belt was a thick bullwhip as it flogged the screaming Bart. Each time the whip left his broad back, a red welt showed itself—and his back was throbbing with muscular reactions as if to greet the next vicious kiss of the whip!

IT WAS WEIRD.

It was bizarre.

It was a scene out of a dungeon of the Middle Ages when brutal lust and love were all one.

The whipmaster was an expert. The blond youth un-doubtedly had been hired by depraved Miami tourists to do this to them as a means of stimulating their masochis-tic urges.

The blond whipmaster worked his way down until he punished Bart's thick buttocks. By now, his body was a se-ries of welts from his shoulders down to his tapering hips.

"Come on," urged the dark-haired boy. "Can't wait all night. Who goes first?"

"Me—me," yelled the blond. "You know I'm the fast-est one."

Bart felt his body grow rigid, then numb. Every fiber of his being was alert. *What were they going to do to him?*

"Hurry up," urged the others. "Nothing like getting it this way—at least he's a good-looking man. Those other queers . . . disgusting . . . not a man among them."

One of them giggled. "Real big, too."

Their passions had become enflamed by the flogging. There were sounds of bottles being opened. They talked as they drank beer.

Suddenly, a heavy pressure was felt by Bart. Naked thighs straddled him around the small of his back.

"W-what . . . ?" he gagged stupidly.

There were no more words spoken. The blond youth's strong body suddenly flattened out. His strong hands gripped both of Bart's muscular buttocks and pulled them apart.

With a horror, Bart knew what was going to happen. It was not true. It was an illusion. It was some nightmare. He would wake up and find it to be a dream.

But no!

It was not a dream.

It was a bizarre Greek tragic-comedy come to life—he was going to be used—just as he had used that girl a few minutes ago. He was being avenged. The gods were laughing. They had won.

A shocking pain ripped through Bart. In a blazing flash of multi-colored fire, Bart felt himself being used like a woman!

A loud roaring erupted into a deafening pounding against his temples. No matter how he struggled, the giggling and laughing trio of youths were going to use him! The blond youth was breathing heavily. Bart remembered how big he was—he was an enviable big male!

Pinching hands gripped his buttocks.

He wanted to scream! He felt himself being ripped apart. Again and again the hammering continued as the blond youth's breathing became more and more pronounced.

Their bodies were bathed in a glow of nervous perspiration. They were like slippery fish.

In a daze, Bart felt his role reversed. Gone were the symbols of his manhood. Gone was his pride. Now he was turned into a woman. The yawning cave refused to yawn to its limit—and the battering ram slammed deeper and deeper. The pain was shocking.

Bart reacted with involuntary spasms. From somewhere, he thought he heard a hoarse laugh and the words, "Lookit that—man—he's acting just like a broad—just like a broad!"

But then the shocking pain softened and what was replaced was the most heavenly feeling Bart thought could exist.

He was swept up in a sea of delicious passion. It was

delight! It was forbidden—shameful—degrading—and this made it all the more delicious!

The blond youth who had mounted Bart now lifted himself up on his elbows. He gave a hoarse cry and suddenly the erotic Gotterdammerung exploded.

Bart nearly screamed—he wanted to laugh, then to sob—it felt hard and fast and so very, very good! His insides were bathed in soul-satisfying lava. Fulfillment was complete.

He was transported on a sea of Nirvana.

Bart was dazed as he felt the blond youth struggle off and could see, from the corner of his eye, the shaky legs— muscular legs with tufts of sun-bleached hair—and then a pair of darker legs straddled Bart. This was the boy with the Beatle haircut.

And then the third boy completed the violation.

Bart had no sense of time. It was as though he were drugged beyond any feeling. Somewhere in the night, he had been released. He was so dazed, he fell into a coma.

When he awakened, it was just early dawn. The beach was deserted. The shrill cries of the white winged gulls vied with the thunderous surf. Dizzily, Bart got up. He looked around. The sands had shifted. He was alone. He felt a stabbing ache and flushed as remembrance returned.

His body still smarted from the flogging. Now, he just wanted to get back home. Despite his nakedness, he made it! It was an experience he would forever remember—it had been a punishment that would have destroyed any man!

But for Bart—it only served to regenerate him!

MONA WAS ALONE NOW. Mel Dalton had gone back to his room at her bidding. He had called her then, called her to tell her that his wife had not yet returned to their room.

"Forget it," Mona told him. "Maybe she's out getting what you just got."

"Not my frigid wife."

"Well, forget her." She laughed. "Maybe she went for a fast swim and got her head nipped off by a shark. Maybe she was crossing the street and got run over by a rented car. Maybe she ran off to Mexico City with a dishwasher. What the hell difference does it make where she is? Mind your own business and go to sleep."

"All right."

"Good night, slave," she said.

"Good night, mistress."

She laughed as she remembered the conversation. What a glorious slave he made! And how marvelous it was to have such utter power over another human being.

It was great.

She slipped out of bed, reached under the bed and removed the tape recorder. The tape had run out long ago. She removed the reel from the machine and put it into its little cardboard box and locked the box away in her strongbox after first labelling it *Mel Dalton–II*. It would make quite a little tape, she knew, and she knew too that she would never blackmail him with it.

What would be the point?

He was her slave already, her slave until she tired of him. She had a hold over him infinitely stronger than the hold that a tape recording of their lovemaking could give her. At her word, he would give her all the money he possessed. At a word from her he would throw himself out of the window. She owned him body and soul, lock stock and barrel, and she didn't have to exert the pressure of blackmail in order to force him to do whatever she chose to ask of him.

All right. She owned him now. But what would she do with him next?

She closed her eyes, rolled over onto her side and tried to sleep. Sleep did not come at once, tired though she was. Her mind kept working, trying to dope out the perfect use for Mel Dalton. There had to be some perfect solution to the question, and it only remained for her to find it.

Oh, a good many amusing pastimes occurred to her at the start. She could have other lovers and make him watch their activity together. She could even force him to go out and bring back men for her. That would be a part of it.

And naturally she would make him leave his wife. He would probably leave his wife sooner or later, in any event, and she could take him away from the frigid broad without any trouble at all. And she would make him sell his business. He had a fairly profitable operation, evidently, and he might even be able to get a good price for it. At her direction, he would sell his business, cash in his life insurance, leave his wife and his apartment, sell his stocks and turn any other holdings he might have into cash. That would give them one hell of a bankroll, and with capital like that at their disposal they could go wherever she wanted to go and do whatever she wanted to do.

Europe. Paris, Rome, London, Florence—wherever she wanted to travel, she would go and he would be at her side, her devoted slave, ready to do whatever she asked of him. Life could be one long holiday for her now simply because she held such unusual and perfect domination over this man.

The sky was the limit. She thought briefly of Bart, the twisted pervert with the horrible ideas, and thought of what he had made her submit to. In a strange sort of way, she knew, she owed it all to Bart. It was his humiliation of her that had nagged at her until she decided to turn the tables and get her revenge by humiliating Mel. And what a brilliant move that had been! Now whole new worlds were opening up for her. She had the world at her feet, just as she had Mel Dalton at her feet. Whatever she wanted would be hers.

She closed her eyes and slept the sleep of the just.

IN HIS OWN BED, Mel Dalton tossed and turned. He too was sleeping, but his sleep was hardly pleasant. He dreamed constantly. He would not remember the dreams when he awoke, but he would know that they had been terrible dreams, awful dreams. All through the night he would toss and turn, waking now and then, gazing around in fear, then dipping once more into a pocket of restless sleep.

He was a victim, caught in a web of female domination, unable to resist, unable to do anything whatsoever to save himself. He was caught. He was saddled and bridled and Mona held the reins. He was bound and gagged, helpless before her. He was the slave, shackled and nailed to the wall, and Mona was his queen, his goddess, his mistress.

In another room, two women slept side by side, their bodies occasionally touching when one of them rolled over in her sleep. Kay lay dreaming of bisexual bliss, of a man and a woman both taking her and possessing her, of the beautiful worlds of lust that opened up to a woman who could accept love from every quarter.

Sue dreamed lesbian dreams. She dreamed of the joys of a life devoid of men, a life where there was an endless procession of female bodies and female breasts and female mouths eager to please her to the hilt. She slept deeply and dreamed beautiful dreams and smiled frequently in her sleep.

And far away on the public beaches to the south, a hollow-eyed man named Bart slept on the sand near the water's edge and dreamed of knives and ropes and screaming female flesh.

Night had come to Miami Beach, the deep dark tail end of night when even the night people crawled into their holes and closed their eyes and gave themselves over to the arms of Morpheus. Night had come, and they all slept now, Mona and Mel and Sue and Kay and Bart, asleep, every last one of them.

They slept.

But dawn would come, bringing with it a new day.

Chapter Thirteen

MEL WOKE EARLY, NOT because he wasn't exhausted but because he woke up coming out of a dream. It was early, not even nine o'clock yet, and he had not gone to sleep until very late and had not slept at all well. He looked at the bed beside him. Sue had not returned to the room during the night. She was gone, had been gone all night long, and he had no idea where she had been or who she might have been with.

He didn't even know if she was alive or dead.

And he couldn't have cared less.

But there was one thing that he did know. He knew that he was literally the slave of Mona. He also knew that this tremendous change in his life could ruin him completely. He had known of men who fell utterly under the spell of some women, and he knew what happened to men like that. They wound up drained and ruined beyond redemption. They wound up crushed. They danced like puppets on strings, until finally the woman who enslaved them cut the strings and let them fall to pieces.

He didn't want that to happen to him. And yet it seemed as though he was powerless to fight it. What could he do? She was his mistress and he was her slave. One word from her was a command to him. She could make him ruin himself, could even force him to kill himself. Last night, when she made him lean out the window until he went nearly insane—well, last night had been proof enough of the hold she had over him. He would have jumped if she told him to. He could not have helped himself.

It was no way for a man to live, no way for him to live, certainly. And he had to find a way out of it. The humiliation he had experienced the night before would be nothing compared to what he would endure later on. He knew this for a fact, and yet—

Wait a minute.

Maybe there was a way out, after all.

He knew instinctively that her hold was a sexual one. If he could break the charm, if he could find sexual release from a source other than Mona, he might stand the ghost of a chance. He had to act quickly, however. If he waited he was doomed. If he hesitated he was lost. If he met her or spoke to her before he had the opportunity to put his plan into action, then he was finished. She would give him an order and he would obey it blindly, and that would be the end of his plan.

But if he could find a woman now, then he had a chance. A good chance, even. He had to take the chance now, had to get out of the hotel before he saw or spoke to Mona. Then he had to find a woman—and for the sake of simplicity he knew that he would be better off picking a woman who would do it for money. A whore, a good old-fashioned whore who would do what had to be done. He'd pay her whatever it cost him. If she could break the chains that made him a slave to Mona, she was worth all the money he had.

He dressed quickly without even bothering to shave. At any moment the phone might ring, and if he answered it, and if it was Mona on the line, then all was lost. Her voice over the telephone had the force to compel him to do anything she asked.

On the way out the door, on the way to the elevator, it occurred to him that maybe he ought to forget it, maybe he ought to stay with Mona. She enslaved him, certainly, but she also yielded him greater pleasure than he had ever known, and—

No!

No, he couldn't let himself start thinking this way. It was nothing short of suicide. If he let himself hear the siren's song, if he let himself be caught in the evil web of her sexual magic, then all was over.

He had to break her power.

And it would take a prostitute to do it.

He rode down to the lobby, hurried out of the hotel, praying that he wouldn't see her on the way. His luck held. He stepped to the curb and managed to hail a cab. He jumped into the back seat, shrank down against the cushions, and told the driver what he wanted.

The driver stared at him. "Whew, buddy," he said, "you must be crazy. You know what time it is?"

"I know."

"It's early in the morning. All the whores in town are sleeping."

"Find one who's willing to wake up."

"But—"

"I don't care what it costs," Mel said. "I don't care about the price. I don't even give much of a damn what the pig looks like. I just want to score."

The cab driver's eyes turned shrewd. "It might cost you a lot of money."

"That's all right."

"Like fifty bucks?"

"Good. And twenty for you if you set it up."

"Seventy total?"

"Fine," Mel said. "Can you find someone?"

"I'm a son of a gun," the cab driver said, putting the cab into gear. "For the kind of money you're paying, Mac, you can get to my wife. Hell, I'll find you somebody. You must be one horny son of a gun, but that's your problem and not mine. I'll find you somebody. Just sit back and hold it in!"

THE CABBY WAS AS good as his word. He drove into Miami proper, heading the cab toward the rundown Cuban neighborhood around the docks. He stopped once, told Mel to stay in the cab. Mel stayed. The cabby came back a few minutes later with a dejected look on his face. "She was asleep," he said. "Dead to the world, all junked up on heroin and on the nod for the next few hours minimum. That's the trouble with trying to find a broad at this hour. But you hold it in, buddy. I'll get you somebody."

He drove two more blocks, parked the cab once more. Mel waited for him. Even now, even this far away in time and space, he could feel the awful attraction of Mona drawing him like a moth to a flame. He wanted to call the whole thing off. This was pretty disgusting, heading for the slums, buying a few moments of professional love from a sleeping, messed-up prostitute.

But he knew better. It wasn't sex he wanted to buy. It was a release, a release from his bondage, bondage that suffocated and overwhelmed him. He didn't much expect to enjoy the sex that the whore would provide. But with luck she might give him the chance to break away from

Mona, and if that happened she was worth whatever she cost, no matter how unpleasant her embrace might be.

When the cabby came back he was smiling. "Done and done," he said. "Go up two flights and it's the room with the door open. The girl's name is Anita. She's a Cuban kid, not bad-looking and young. She knows her way around pretty good, too. You got to give her fifty bucks. That's twenty you owe me, plus what's on the meter. Makes it twenty-two seventy-five."

Mel handed him three ten-dollar bills. "You can keep the change," he told the driver. "But how about waiting for me to get through so you can run me back to the hotel."

"Fair enough."

"I won't be long."

The driver chuckled. "You take all the time you want, Mac," he said. "You're paying enough for it."

Mel got out of the cab and headed into the ramshackle tenement the driver had indicated. The building had been a mess when it was built, and the years had not been kind to it. The hallways stank of Spanish cooking odors mingled with the smells of cheap wine, stale urine, and human excrement of various persuasions. The stench was so thick that he had trouble getting up the two flights of stairs. At the third floor he looked around until he saw one door wide open. He hesitated at the threshold, then took a step inside.

A girl was waiting, a professional smile on her young face. One look told Mel that she couldn't have been more than seventeen at the most. Another look told him that it didn't matter how young or old she was. She had been around plenty. Her eyes had the wisdom born of too many nights on a cheap mattress with a man between her girlish thighs. Young or not, she knew what it was all about.

She was attractive, too. Her skin was the color of good coffee with plenty of cream in it. She was wearing a cheap red bathrobe, and it didn't take X-ray vision to guess that there was nothing under the robe but the girl herself. Anita, he reminded himself. That was her name. Anita.

"You have the money, meester?"

He started to hand her a fifty, then realized that she might have trouble cashing it. He counted out five ten-dollar bills and handed them to her. Her eyes widened at the sight of so much money. He guessed that she was probably lucky to earn ten bucks in a whole night. She snatched the bills from him greedily and hurried to stuff them in the bottom drawer of the old bureau. Then she turned toward him, smiling once more, and she took off her robe.

She had a fine body. Her breasts, while quite small, were perfectly formed; they protruded from her chest with the fresh bloom of youth. Her stomach was flat as a flounder, her private parts almost hairless. She moved to the bed with an inborn easy grace and lay down on it with perfect ease.

Mel looked at her. She was lovely, and he recognized the fact, but this didn't do anything for him. He felt no quickening spasm of desire, no sweet lustful tension. He looked at her and felt nothing at all.

IT WOULD COME, HE knew. And he got out of his own clothes quickly and joined her on the bed. Her flesh was warm from sleep. She had a fine musty smell to her. He touched her, and she took him in her arms and kissed him on the mouth. His hands moved to her breasts and she pretended to respond, moving softly beneath him and making tiny sounds down deep in her throat.

Nothing.

He touched her thighs, and he felt her small hands groping to touch him. She held him and toyed with him, and he touched all the special parts of her lush young body.

Nothing.

Nothing at all.

He kept trying, forcing himself to handle her with passion, forcing himself out of sheer desperation. He was afraid now. He knew what it meant if he failed. He knew what kind of a life he could look forward to if this young Cuban girl failed to set him aflame with desire. He knew that it would indicate that he was Mona's slave forever, that he had no hope of escape this side of the grave.

Still nothing happened.

Finally, she seemed to know that it was not going to work. She pushed him and he rolled away from her, sick inside, sick in his heart. He was through. Life from this point on would be nothing but Hell. His work, his life— all of it, shattered forever, shattered beyond repair.

"MEESTER," SHE SAID, "notting is happening."

"I know."

"Maybe we try something else, okay?"

He didn't know what she meant.

"Sometimes a man gets a little trouble," she said sagely. "One ting always fixes him up, you know? I try and we see what happens, okay?"

"Sure," he said.

And then she was crouching over him, down at the foot of the bed, and he knew what it was that she meant. He looked up and saw her little rosebud mouth, her lips, her tongue, and she sought him and found him, and his heart overflowed at the sight of her youth giving itself up in this most intimate of caresses.

She did her work very well. She taught him tricks he had never even known about, slaved over him, gave him the ultimate in honey love, but it was useless.

Nothing happened.

Nothing.

And at last, she gave up. She had a very unhappy expression on her face, partly because she was genuinely sorry that she had failed to satisfy him, partly because she feared he might try to make trouble for her. Sometimes men were apt to do that when they couldn't make love. They acted as though it was the girl's fault, no matter how hard she had tried to accommodate them, and they tried to take their money back.

But he had no intention of doing anything like that. It wasn't Anita's fault that he was captive to another woman, so much so that he could not be moved to respond to anyone on earth but Mona. It wasn't Anita's fault and he had no reason to be angry with her. If anything, he was ashamed of himself, embarrassed at his impotence. He dressed quickly and left her room and hurried through the foul-smelling building to the street outside.

The cab driver was waiting. He had an admiring smile for Mel. "I got to give you credit." he said. "You were with her for close to an hour, and that's real stamina. Most guys can't go more than five minutes with Anita. She's a little tiger, the way she twitches that tail of hers. Gets a man's rocks off almost before he drops his pants."

So, the cabby thought he had been making love all the time. Actually, he had merely struck out. Struck out?

Hell, he had never been able to get his bat off his shoulder. He had watched three pitches sail by, and that was the end of it.

Well, there was no sense correcting the cabby, he thought. He had had enough embarrassment for the day. He let the cabby drive him back to the Banzai, gave him an unnecessary extra ten bucks for the ride back, and walked into the lobby.

His shoulders sagged as he walked. He took the elevator to his floor and let himself into his room. Sue had returned, evidently. Some of her clothes were draped over a chair, and they had not been there before. But she was gone now. Not that he cared. Not that he gave a damn about her, or anyone else.

Except Mona.

He went to the bathroom. He looked in the mirror over the sink and almost failed to recognize himself. His face was puffy. There were pouches under his eyes, and he needed a shave desperately, and his whole face had a downcast look to it that spelled nothing but defeat.

He sagged completely. He was a broken man, a beaten man, a wasted man, and he was through.

Chapter Fourteen

Maybe she was crazy.

At first, when she woke up, Sue Dalton thought that she would get Kay to run off with her. She had it all worked out in her mind. They could go far away—to San Francisco, maybe, or almost anywhere. They could find an apartment. She would get work—she didn't want Mel's money, didn't want any contact with him. And the two of them could live together.

When she told Kay about it, the older woman reached for her wordlessly, and they made love. It was slow and gentle and beautiful, and Sue thought that this was Kay's way of agreeing to the plan. She lay silent next to Kay after the crescendo of orgasm had receded, and she learned, much to her surprise, that this was not Kay's way of agreeing to the plan.

It was Kay's way of turning her down.

"There are a few things you have to understand about me," Kay told her. "In the first place, I'm not a lesbian."

"Sure," she said, certain that Kay was kidding. Obviously Kay was a lesbian—what did Kay think they had just been doing? Playing Parcheesi?

"I'm not."

"Sure. You're really the Queen of Romania."

"No, but I happen to be bisexual."

"You mean—"

"I mean I enjoy it with men, but I also enjoy it with women as well. Either way is just as much fun for me."

"I don't believe it."

"It's true."

"But . . . but you and I are perfect together. I can't believe that you could want a man after what you and I do together."

Kay smiled lazily. "Maybe you won't believe this either. But after we . . . made love last night, well, I couldn't sleep, dear. I was restless and I couldn't sleep, so I got up and left you here and went out."

"I know that."

"Oh?"

"I woke up and saw that you were gone. I was afraid you might pick up some other girl."

"I picked up a man."

"You—"

"Yes, Sue. I went down on the beach and a man found me and made love to me."

Her mind reeled. She might have been unable to accept the story if it weren't for the fact that she knew it was true—Kay had left her that night, and the rest of the story followed logically enough from that. She listened as Kay went on to explain her own special sexuality, how she got along with men as well as women, how she could not see any reason why she should limit herself as long as she enjoyed whatever she did. And, finally, Kay described in gory detail what the filthy man named Bart had done to her on the beach the night before. It sounded so horrible that Sue was sick. She couldn't imagine how Kay could possibly have enjoyed it, but the older woman merely smiled and assured her that different things were enjoyable to different people.

Which seemed logical enough.

But the whole revelation certainly dashed her plans to smithereens. Obviously she couldn't expect Kay to come running off to some little love nest with her. In her mind she had managed to magnify her affair with Kay to the point where it seemed like a real romance. But it was nothing of the kind. It was simply the case of a strong sexual attraction that had led to a relationship which both of them had found quite enjoyable.

Now it was over. But this did not mean either that she ought to stay with Mel. Whether or not Kay came with her, her mind was very clear on that point. She had to get away, had to go off somewhere by herself. She would build an entirely new life for herself in some city where she did not know a soul and where she had never been before. She thought again of San Francisco. Why not? There was no particular place that she preferred. She could go there. She could find an apartment. She could discover the places where the gay girls lived and loved, and she could at long last begin to live the life that was right for her.

She called her own room from Kay's room. There was no answer. She let the phone ring a long time to make sure that Mel was really out, that he was not simply asleep. Then she said goodbye to Kay and hurried down to her room, changed to clean clothes, tossed a few of her better dresses and all of her jewelry into her suitcase, and left the hotel without further ado.

She had enough money—nearly four hundred dollars in her purse, plus several thousand dollars worth of jewelry that Mel had given her over the years. The jewelry would sell for a good price. The money it brought would sustain her until she found work and give her a cushion to lean on. There was no reason to try to get more money out of Mel. If she ever needed it, she could always divorce him and get her hooks into him for some alimony, but in the meantime she could live without that kind of money.

Just so she had plenty of love.

She took a cab to the airport. It seemed incredible that she had been at that airport less than twenty-four hours earlier, arriving in Miami then instead of departing from it. In less than a full day so much had happened, so very much, and her life had changed so utterly and completely. It was almost impossible to believe all that had happened, and all in such a short span of time.

Now a new world was opening up for her. She could live the way she had always craved to live, the way she had never dared to live. Never again would she have to put up with the embraces of a man. Never again would she have to sneak around hunting for love. Never again would she have to pretend to be something that she wasn't, or hide what she was. And she was going off on her own, without a soul for company, determined to look out for herself.

She went to the airline ticket counter. There was a flight leaving for San Francisco at two in the afternoon.

When it left, she was on it.

IN A WAY, KAY was sorry to see her go. Sue Dalton had been good company in bed and out of bed, a fine warm lovely young woman who was born for a special kind of love. She would have enjoyed seeing more of her, would have enjoyed having her around for a few more days, even for a week.

Yet she knew well enough that it was better this way. Sue had a life to live, and she had the right to live it to the hilt. For far too long she had been wasting herself, living with a man when she should have been living with women, seeking furtively after love when she should have been able to make love openly and sanely. So, Sue had to break away, and Sue was the type of woman who needed to make the break violently, on the spur of the moment. She couldn't tell her husband, couldn't get involved in long legal wrangles, couldn't just work her way out of her marriage inch by inch. She had to do it all at once, and now, fortunately, she had finally gotten up the guts to do it.

So, Kay was happy for her.

And Kay was happy for Kay. The trip to Miami had thus far been vastly rewarding, and she planned to stay for another two weeks before she took off for some other place. Already she had found two lovers, each perfect on his or own terms. Sue—a woman. And Bart—a brutal man.

She shivered at the memory of Bart. He had terrified her. He had hurt her, so much so that parts of her body still ached. She could feel the pain of his embrace in memory just by thinking about it. Yet the fact remained that no one had ever thrilled her quite so profoundly as he had done. No doubt the novelty of his way of lust was at least partially responsible for the vitality of her response. Even so, it had been a wild and wonderful experience, and she was glad she had taken part in it.

Would she see him again? Probably not, she knew. She might go down to the beaches every night, and even so he would probably never return to the spot while she was there. It was a shame, but she was used to loving people and leaving them, so it was nothing new. She thought of all the lovers she had had, men and women both, and how over the course of time each and every one of them had vanished completely from her life.

Easy come, she thought.

And easy go.

She called down to room service and ordered an extravagant lunch—imported caviar, a vodka martini, a cold lobster platter, chef salad with Roquefort dressing, and black coffee. The boy who wheeled in her tray was very young, with a deep tan and a temptingly thin body. She flirted shamelessly with him while he prepared the table, and she knew he would be back for more.

She drank her martini and felt its effect at once. She had a great appetite. She wolfed down the caviar and the lobster platter and the salad, washing everything down with several cups of hot black coffee.

Then she took off all her clothes and put on a sheer, black negligee. She sprayed cologne under her arms and between her breasts and legs.

When the youthful waiter returned, he didn't stand the chance of a snowball in hell. She coaxed him out of his clothes and into her bed, and she climaxed a perfect meal by gobbling him up for dessert.

MEL KNELT AT THE foot of the bed, his hands folded in supplication. This was part of the pattern, he knew. And the pattern was one he would never be able to break. It would go on forever until one of them died. He was trapped, enslaved, and there was nothing to be done about it. He had had his chance with the little Cuban prostitute in downtown Miami. He had tried his best, and so had the girl, and absolutely nothing had happened.

He knew it was his last chance. Now Mona had him by the short hairs. Her hold on him would do nothing but increase every day of his life.

Her voice: "Who are you?"

"I am your slave."

"Who am I?"

"You are my queen."

"What will you do for me?"

"Anything."

"Anything?"

"Anything."

"Should I be merciful to you?"

"Please," he begged.

Her laughter cut like a knife. "Oh, I don't think I will, Mel. I'm just not cut out for mercy. You're going to leave your wife, Mel. Did you know that?"

"I know."

"You're going to sell your business."

"All right."

"Do you have much money in stocks? I want you to convert it all into cash."

"All right."

"And real estate? Sell it all."

"All right."

"And you must have life insurance policies. You'll have to cash them in."

"Yes."

"I'll want every penny of your money. When you want money, you will have to ask me for it. Do you understand?"

"I understand."

"If you're a good boy," she said, "maybe I'll let you have a few dollars when you ask. If you're not, I'll be just as wicked."

"I understand." Oh, he understood all right. He understood everything. She was going to run his life, and she was going to ruin his life, and he was helpless before her. He had worked like a dog to build up a business. Now he would be locked into selling out to his partner for a fraction of what the place was really worth. But she didn't want a business. She wanted money, and he had no choice but to give it to her.

"Do you love me, slave?"

"Yes."

"Do you want me?"

"Yes."

"Right now?"

"Yes."

"Stand up. Let me see."

He stood up and she studied him.

"All right," she said. She was smiling, but her voice had lost none of its hardness. "You've been a good boy, slave. Come and get your reward."

And, hating himself and hating her as well, he went to her and took his cup of pleasure.

THE MAN IN THE lunch counter sat at a stool watching a cup of coffee get cold in front of him. The waitress came over to ask him if anything was the matter with the coffee. He looked up at her and met her eyes with his. Her eyes were blue, her hair blonde, and her figure a little on the chunky side. She had nice breasts, he noticed. Big as basketballs.

"The coffee's fine," he said.

"It must be cold. You want me to heat it up for you?"

Always playing up to a man, he thought. They were all like that, little teasers who did anything they could to play up to a man because they were all dirty, they all stank inside and out, they all reeked of rotten fish.

He smiled. His smile was handsome, with white teeth

flashing in his deeply tanned face. His eyes, sunk deep into his head, were striking. The girl smiled back in spite of herself.

He leaned forward. "Forget the coffee," he said persuasively. "Listen to me. What time do you get through here?"

"Why . . . uh . . . four o'clock. Why?"

"I'll pick you up."

"Well—"

"C'mon," he said. He was very handsome when he smiled, and he knew it. He reached for her hand now. He took her hand in one of his and used the index finger of his other hand to trace a brace of tiny circles on her palm.

"Four o'clock," he said.

"All right."

"Do you have a car?"

"Yes."

"Because I don't. Fine. We'll take your car, and I'll pick you up at four o'clock."

He didn't wait for an answer, just swung off his stool and left the little luncheonette. Filthy bitches, he thought. Rotten, every last one of them. But this one would be fun. He knew that she would be fun.

Bart smiled. All the girls in Miami were fun, he thought, and his smile widened.

Bart was very handsome when he smiled.

Chapter Fifteen

When the plane landed in San Francisco, Sue Dalton was the first one off it. She had her suitcase in her hand. She had not checked any baggage. She walked through the terminal and outside to where the taxis were waiting. She started to head for one of the cabs, then realized that she was not sure where she wanted to be taken. She went back inside the terminal and over to along line of telephone booths. She looked under Hotels in the Yellow Pages. A hotel called the Seabrook had a very large display ad, and looked as though it would be decent enough. She didn't care much about price, just so long as she had a decent place to stay. If it was too expensive she could always move elsewhere in a day or two.

She called the Seabrook, and asked if they had a vacant single. They did, for $12.50 a day, which was fine. She made a reservation as Sue Miles. Her maiden name, she thought, and there was no reason why she shouldn't use it again. It sounded a hell of a lot better than Sue Dalton.

She went back to the line of cabs and got into one of them, asking the driver to take her to the Seabrook Hotel. He nodded and pulled the taxi away from the curb.

She relaxed and looked out the window.

It had been afternoon when she left Miami. It was still afternoon, and, in fact, it was a few minutes earlier than it had been when her plane had left Miami. The time zones were such that a jet could land in San Francisco before it had left Miami. Strange, she thought, smiling, and she adjusted her watch accordingly. The watch had been a gift from Mel, which, she thought, meant that she would want to sell it sooner or later, just as she intended to convert every last one of his gifts into cash. She wanted no physical memories of the man who had been her husband. She was starting life anew, starting life once more as Sue Miles instead of Sue Dalton, and this time she wanted to do it right.

"We're here, Miss."

The cabby's words broke in upon her reverie. She looked up at the Hotel Seabrook. It was impressive, with high columns at the doorway and a liveried doorman opening the cab door for her and reaching for her suitcase. She paid the cabby, tipped him, and followed the doorman through the hotel lobby to the registration desk. She signed a card and took her key and went over to the elevator and up to the eighth floor with a bellhop. The bellhop showed her into her room, checked soap and towels, opened a window and smiled his thanks for the dollar she gave him. Then, alone in her room, she quickly unpacked her suitcase and tried to decide what to do next.

There were plenty of gay bars in San Francisco, she knew. And you didn't have to be a genius to find them. The North Beach area, where the beatnik types hung out, was supposed to be crawling with gay boys and lesbians. And the downtown area around and off of Market Street was supposed to be just as good for cruising. All she had to do was find the right bar and make the right connections, and before she knew what was happening she would be in the swim of things, a charter member of the gay crowd.

Why not?

She undressed, showered quickly. She was tired and the bed was inviting, but her desire for sleep was nothing at all compared to her desire for something a lot more exciting than sleep. She wanted sex, and she wanted it soon, and sleep could wait.

But first she had to find somebody. She dressed conservatively but attractively in a tight black skirt and a beige sweater that hugged her body and showed her breasts to best effect. She clutched her purse, locked her door from the outside, dropped her key into her purse, and left the hotel.

It didn't take her long.

Not long at all. She found a bar on Caspar Avenue that looked promising, but nothing happened there and she left after two dry bourbon Manhattans. She moved down Caspar to Orange and over Orange to Michaelson Street, and there she found a bar called Allemande Left, and the minute she opened the door she knew at once that she was in the right place. There was not a man in the bar. Just girls, and all of them obviously gay.

Two girls danced in the rear to music from the juke box, their bodies pressed invitingly together, their hips swaying slowly together in time to the music. At a back booth, one girl was rubbing another girl's thigh.

This place was the real thing, she thought. Even the gay bars in New York had not gone this far. The dancing, the open petting—the Allemande Left was pretty far out, all right. And it was just right for her, because she was in the mood and ready to go. She didn't care who saw her, didn't have to worry about word getting back to her husband. Because as far as she was concerned she didn't have a husband any more. She wanted to have a good time, and having a good time was certainly the only thing that mattered.

At the bar she ordered another Manhattan. The barmaid was a butch type with short hair and broad shoulders and virtually no breasts at all. She mixed the drink expertly and set it on the bar top in front of Sue.

"You're new here," she said.

"I just hit town an hour ago."

"You found the right place, didn't you?"

"I certainly hope so."

The barmaid's pink tongue came out, licked her thin lips. "A doll like you won't have trouble," she said. "I'd like to give you a whirl myself."

"One of these days."

"You know it, baby." The barmaid winked and scurried off to service another customer. Sue smiled a private smile to herself. No trouble at all, she told herself. And maybe she would take a stab at the barmaid sooner or later. Hell, she thought. Sooner or later, she would go to bed with every lesbian in San Francisco.

A voice said, "Hello, you."

She turned. The girl who had spoken stood close to six feet tall. She was broad-shouldered and thick in the waist, and she looked like a truckdriver except for her huge protruding breasts. She wore tight slacks and a man's shirt with a button-down collar. She put a hand on Sue's shoulder and winked.

"You in the mood?"

Sue smiled. "Maybe."

"No games, now. My doll went around the corner but she'll be back in maybe ten minutes. We got time for a little fun in the meanwhile, but we can't fool around. Yes or no, girl."

"Well—"

"Yes or no."

She had never been the target of an approach like this. Sex, pure and simple, she thought. No preliminaries, no friendliness, just a cold proposition. She wouldn't care for this sort of thing as a steady diet, but at the moment it seemed oddly exciting.

Why not? She had nothing better to do, and after the little interlude with the big stocky dyke she could see about finding someone more refined for the rest of the evening.

"All right," she said. "But where?"

The dyke squeezed her shoulder. "Go on into the john," she said. "The ladies' room. I'll be in in a minute."

A STRANGE PLACE FOR a romantic dalliance, she thought. But she didn't protest. She got off her stool and went to the bathroom at the back of the bar. It was a small, foul-smelling cubicle, one dim bulb dangling from the ceiling, with deodorizer smells struggling to cancel out the smells of human excrement.

The door opened. The dyke came inside, and closed the door and bolted it.

"Take off your skirt," she ordered.

"But—"

"A tight skirt like that, you can't just pull it up. Better take it off."

She took off her skirt.

"Panties, yet," the dyke said. "You might as well have come in a goddam suit of armor. Take off the panties, honey. Let's see how sweet and lovely you are."

No preliminaries at all, she thought. No caresses, nothing, and surroundings like this, filthy and depressing. Still there was no denying the naked need that trembled in her loins.

She look off her panties.

"Now sit down. On the pot, honey."

She sat on the toilet seat, feeling slightly ridiculous. She was nude from the waist down. The dyke looked her over and smiled lustfully and then, at once, sank to the ground and stayed in front of Sue on her knees.

"Nice," the dyke said. "Nice and pretty and sweet. Now come to Mommy, little girl."

And then the dyke stopped talking.

At first Sue didn't enjoy it. At first she couldn't block the coldness of it out of her mind, nor could she entirely disregard the smell of the lavatory, the sterileness of the surroundings. But the dyke knew what she was doing and did it damn well. Sue's thighs were moist with the dew of love. Her body began to tremble. Her loins bloomed from the girl's kisses.

And then she forgot certain things. She forgot that she was sitting in a pigsty of a lavatory, sitting on the edge of a toilet with an unattractive girl kneeling before her. She forgot too that the girl did not care for her and that she did not care for the girl. She forgot the coldness of the girl's approach, forgot how sheerly physical it all was. She forgot all of this and she gave herself up entirely to the bath of oral sensations that flooded over her thighs and groin, and the world began to spin faster, faster and faster, and she felt herself throbbing and trembling, faster and harsher and wilder, and everything went into a dazzling tailspin and the dyke drained her, swallowed her up and digested her, and bang bang bang she went off like a bomb.

"You're a tasty one," the dyke said. "Get dressed now, honey. Put your pants and skirt on and go have yourself another drink. I got to get out of here, now. My girl gets jealous as hell when I cheat on her. But you're worth it. You're a sweet one, you really are, baby."

The dyke left without even rinsing her mouth. Sue struggled to her feet, managed to gain her balance. She put on her pants and her skirt and inspected herself in the mirror. She had deep circles of gratified desire under her eyes.

She went out of the john and had another drink.

MEL DALTON WAS IN the closet. He was in Mona's closet, to be quite accurate. The closet door was closed, and the closet light was off, and he crouched in the darkness. Waiting.

There was a peephole in the door. Mona had drilled the hole for him that afternoon, explaining that no one would notice it. He had to stand in the closet and look through the peephole while Mona amused herself with other lovers. It made him sick to think about it, but there was nothing to do about it. He had to do whatever she told him to do, and she had told him to do this, and so he had no choice at all.

"Maybe you'll like it," she had said. "Lots of men like to watch, you know. It's fun."

"Mona—"

"You love me, don't you?"

"Yes."

"Well, then you can watch other men loving me. It should be a special treat for you."

"Mona—"

But she insisted, and there was nothing he could do, nothing at all. If she told him to do something he had no choice but to do it just as she said. Now he was waiting in the closet, and soon she would return with someone, and he would have to watch.

He heard sounds, movement in the hallway. A key turned in a lock and lights went on inside the room. He listened to the voices, Mona's voice and some man's voice. He pressed his face to the door, his eye to the peephole, and when they came into view he saw them both.

Mona, his Mona, his goddess, his enslaver. Already she was taking her clothes off, laughing as she did so. And with her, the man—scarcely more than a boy, really, thin and hungry-looking, his desire easy to read in his innocent eyes.

They both undressed completely.

They got onto the bed.

And Mel watched.

What he watched was unlike anything he had ever seen or done or heard of. It was dirty, depraved, perverted, and he thought that Mona was worse than he had ever imagined, that she was corrupting the youth of the boy, ruining him just as surely as she had ruined Mel, if in a different way. He wanted to tear his eye from the peephole, wanted to stop watching, wanted to do his utmost to stop even thinking about what was going on before him.

It was no use. She had told him to watch, and nothing could make him stop following her orders. He watched for what seemed like an eternity, watched as Mona had her obscene way with the boy, watched for almost forever until at last they were through and the boy rolled away from her with a sickly moan and, finally, got into his clothing without a word and left.

He stayed in the closet.

Waiting.

And her voice called to him. "Come out now, Mel," she was calling. "He's gone, slave. Come out now. Come out on your knees, Mel."

He opened the door. He looked at her, both hating her and loving her, and he fell to his knees.

"Crawl to me, Mel."

He crawled to her.

"Ah, Mel," she said. "He was a sweet boy, wasn't he? And very good, you know. I think I showed him some things he had never known before. Isn't that nice?"

He couldn't answer her.

"Do you want me, now? Do you want to make love to me, Mel? Do you, slave?"

NO, his brain shrieked. But his lips said, "Yes, Mona. Yes, I want you."

And he did want her. That was the worst part of all. He wanted her so much he ached.

"I think I'll make you wait awhile," she said. "You've been a good boy, but I'll make you wait a little while anyway." She yawned and stretched. "In the meantime, I think I'll let you wash my feet, Mel. My feet are dirty, and I've always liked having them washed for me."

He started to go to the bathroom for a washcloth. "No," she said, laughing at him. "Not with a cloth. Use your tongue, Mel."

And slave that he was, he bent to this task.

MY NEWSLETTER: I get out an email newsletter at unpredictable intervals, but rarely more often than every other week. I'll be happy to add you to the distribution list. A blank email to lawbloc@gmail.com with "newsletter" in the subject line will get you on the list, and a click of the "Unsubscribe" link will get you off it, should you ultimately decide you're happier without it.

LAWRENCE BLOCK is a Mystery Writers of America Grand Master. His work over the past half century has earned him multiple Edgar Allan Poe and Shamus awards, the U.K. Diamond Dagger for lifetime achievement, and recognition in Germany, France, Taiwan, and Japan. His latest novel is *Dead Girl Blues*; other recent fiction includes *A Time to Scatter Stones, Keller's Fedora*, and *The Burglar in Short Order*. In addition to novels and short fiction, he has written episodic television (*Tilt!*) and the Wong Kar-wai film, *My Blueberry Nights*.

Block contributed a fiction column in Writer's Digest for fourteen years, and has published several books for writers, including the classic *Telling Lies for Fun & Profit* and the updated and expanded *Writing the Novel from Plot to Print to Pixel*. His nonfiction has been collected in *The Crime of Our Lives* (about mystery fiction) and *Hunting Buffalo with Bent Nails* (about everything else). Most recently, his collection of columns about stamp collecting, *Generally Speaking*, has found a substantial audience throughout and far beyond the philatelic community.

Lawrence Block has lately found a new career as an anthologist (*At Home in the Dark*; *From Sea to Stormy Sea*) and holds the position of writer-in-residence at South Carolina's Newberry College. He is a modest and humble fellow, although you would never guess as much from this biographical note.

Email: lawbloc@gmail.com
Twitter: @LawrenceBlock
Facebook: lawrence.block
Website: lawrenceblock.com

www.ingramcontent.com/pod-product-compliance
Lightning Source LLC
Chambersburg PA
CBHW061522120726
48001CB00004B/1387